American Folktales, II

Crowell Contemporary
English Series

Virginia French Allen
People in Livingston
People in Fact and Fiction

Virginia F. Allen and Robert L. Allen
Review Exercises for English as a Foreign Language

Robert L. Allen, Virginia F. Allen, and Margaret Shute
English Sounds and Their Spellings

Daniel da Cruz, Jr.
Men Who Made America

Vinal O. Binner
American Folktales/I and *II: A Structured Reader*
International Folktales/I and *II: A Structured Reader*

Sara Withers
The United Nations in Action: A Structured Reader

Margaret Kurilecz
Man and His World: A Structured Reader

Institute of Modern Languages, Inc.
Contemporary Spoken English I–V
Contemporary Review Exercises I–II

George P. McCallum
Idiom Drills

American Folktales, II

A Structured Reader

Vinal O. Binner

Thomas Y. Crowell Company   New York   Established 1834

R-W-RK

ACKNOWLEDGMENTS

For permission to adapt copyrighted stories for this reader, acknowledgment is extended to the following:

J. R. Aswell, Julia Wilhoit, Jennette Edwards, E. Miller, and Lena E. Lipscomb, of the Tennessee Writers' Project, "Little Eight John" and "Young Melvin," from *God Bless the Devil*. By permission of The University of North Carolina Press, Chapel Hill.

J. Frank Dobie, "The Judge," adapted from "Senor Coyote Acts as Judge," in *Coyote Wisdom*. By permission of the Texas Folklore Society.

Zora Neale Hurston, "Jim and the Angel" and "Good Shooting," from *Mules and Men*, J. B. Lippincott Co. Copyright 1920 by Zora Neale Hurston. By permission of Clifford J. Hurston and John C. Hurston.

M. A. Jagendorf, "The Unlucky Wedding Day," adapted from "True Love in the Blue Mountains." Reprinted by permission of the publisher, The Vanguard Press, Inc., from *Upstate, Downstate: Folk Stories of the Middle Atlantic States* by M. A. Jagendorf. Copyright 1949 by M. A. Jagendorf.

Edward L. Keithahn, "The Hunter and the Raven," from *Igloo Tales*, September, 1945. By permission of Robert D. Seal Publications, Seattle, Washington.

THOMAS Y. CROWELL COMPANY
666 FIFTH AVENUE
NEW YORK, N.Y. 10019

Preface

The units in this text continue in progression of difficulty from those in *American Folktales I: A Structured Reader*. Nearly 400 new vocabulary words and 225 idioms have been added. The arrangement of material is the same as in the first volume.

Those classes desiring explanations as well as practice in the learning of grammar will find the Glossary of Grammatical Terms, on page 125, helpful.

Contents

x *Contents*

Unit 1

The Ghost Cats

An old preacher was riding on his horse through the country. When night came, he began to look everywhere for a place to stop. Because there were so many clouds in the sky the night was very dark, and he became a little bit nervous. But after a time he saw a light. He rode toward it, and soon he saw that it came from a small house.

When he reached the house, the preacher got off his horse. He tied it to a fence post in the front yard. Then he went up to the house and knocked on the door.

1

A man opened the door and said, "Good evening, preacher."

"Good evening," said the preacher. "I'm lost. May I stay at your house tonight? I can sleep anywhere."

"I want to help you, preacher," said the man, "but I have a wife and ten children. There's no place here for you to sleep."

The old preacher slowly crossed the front yard. He untied his horse and got on it. Then he started to ride away.

The man called from the doorway, "Preacher, you can sleep in the big house down the road. Nobody lives there, and the door is open. You can put your horse in the barn and feed it, and inside the house is some wood, so you can make a fire and be comfortable."

"Oh, thank you!" said the preacher, and he began to ride away down the dark road.

"But, preacher," the man called, "I hope you don't care. That house has ghosts."

The preacher hesitated, but then he rode on. He did not want to see any ghosts, but there was no other place for him to stay.

Finally he got to the big house. He put his horse in the barn and gave it something to eat. Then he went to the door of the house and pushed against it with his hand. It was open. In the biggest room he found a large fireplace with a lot of wood in it. He put a match to the wood, and soon there was a big fire.

As the room became warm, the old preacher sat down near the fire in a comfortable chair. Then he took a book from his coat and began to read. The fire was hot and bright.

Suddenly, as the old man sat reading his book, there was a noise in one corner of the room. The preacher looked up and saw a big black cat. The cat moved slowly across the room. It walked to the fire and lay down on the burning wood. It looked at the man with its big green eyes. Then it left the fire, walked over to him, and sat down near his feet. It put out its red tongue, moved its tail back and forth, and said, "Wait until Emmett comes."

The old man wanted to leave, but he pretended to read his book. Suddenly he heard a noise somewhere else in the room. He looked up and saw another black cat. It was as big as a dog. It moved slowly across the room, went to the fire, and lay down in it. Then it sat down beside the first cat, near the man, put out its long red tongue, and moved its tail back and forth. "What shall we do with him?" it asked the first cat.

"Wait until Emmett comes," the first cat answered.

The old man tried to read his book. After a time he heard another noise in another corner of the room. He looked up and saw a cat as big as a cow and as black as the night. It, too, walked slowly across the room to the fire. There it sat down and ate some of the burning wood. After that, it came over to the man and stood in front of him. It looked at him with its big green eyes, put out its long hot tongue, moved its heavy tail back and forth, and asked the other cats, "What shall we do with him?"

"Wait until Emmett comes," they answered.

The preacher looked around the room for Emmett, and he was glad that he didn't see him. He closed his book and put it back into his coat. Then he said, "Well, friends, I'm glad to meet you. You're nice cats. But when Emmett comes, tell him I *was* here but I went away."

Then the old man ran as fast as he could to his horse and rode away into the dark night.

Vocabulary

anywhere	everywhere	to hesitate	somewhere
barn	fence	inside	tail
blank	fireplace	to knock	unhappy
cloud	forth	match	to untie
comfortable	ghost	nowhere	

Idioms

to put a match to
back and forth

Related Words

cloud (noun)
cloudy (adj.)

comfortable (adj.)
comfort (noun)
comfortably (adv.)

to knock (verb)
knocker (noun)

unhappy (adj.)
unhappiness (noun)

Opposites

comfortable—uncomfortable
inside—outside
to leave—to arrive (at)
unhappy—happy
to untie—to tie

Structure

I. THE ADVERBS <u>ANYWHERE</u>, <u>EVERYWHERE</u>, <u>SOME-WHERE</u>, AND <u>NOWHERE</u>

A. *Anywhere may be used in interrogative, negative, and some affirmative sentences:*

Do you want to go **anywhere**?
   No, I don't want to go **anywhere**.
   You may sit down **anywhere** you want.

B. *<u>Somewhere</u> may be used in an interrogative or affirmative sentence:*

Did you go **somewhere** that was interesting?

I put my pen **somewhere** in this room.

C. *Everywhere may be used in an interrogative, negative, or affirmative sentence:*

Did you look **everywhere** for your pen?

No, I didn't look **everywhere**.

Yes, I think I looked **everywhere** in the house.

D. *Nowhere is a negative word. It is never used in the same sentence as* not:

I went **nowhere** yesterday.

Or, I did **not** go **anywhere** yesterday.

E. *Complete the following sentences by filling in each blank with* anywhere, *somewhere,* everywhere, *or* nowhere.

1. He lost his book _____.
2. He can't find it _____.
3. There are people _____ in the country.
4. I need to go _____ to rest.
5. I go _____ by airplane, but _____ by car.
6. The poor hungry man has _____ to go.
7. Are you going _____ tomorrow?
8. No, but I'm going _____ on Tuesday.
9. From a ship, you can see water _____.
10. It's raining here, but _____ the sun is shining.

II. STATEMENTS CONNECTED BY BUT AND BUT . . . NOT

A. *A sentence stating that one person is doing something, and a second person is not, is often made as follows:*

John is studying, **but** Bill is **not**.

B. *When one person does not do something and the second person does, the sentence may be made as follows:*

John is not studying, **but** Bill is.

Structure (**continued**)

C. *Read aloud each of the following sentences:*

The cats stayed, **but** the preacher did **not.**
The preacher read a book, **but** the cats did **not.**
I am learning English, **but** my sister is **not.**
He did not sit in the fire, **but** they did.
He does not come to class, **but** I do.

D. *Complete the following sentences by giving the correct form of each verb in parentheses. One verb in each of the sentences will be affirmative, the other negative:*

Example: He _____ (knock) _____ on the door, but his friend did.

He did not knock on the door, but his friend did.

1. The horse _____ (be) _____ in the barn, but the cats are not.
2. She _____ (be) _____ happy, but I am.
3. These desks are uncomfortable, but the others _____ (be) _____.
4. He likes the book, but his father _____ (do) _____.
5. We _____ (work) _____, but they are not.
6. She fussed, but he _____ (do) _____.
7. One dog buried its bone, but the other _____ (do) _____.
8. I _____ (stand) _____ by the door, but Mary did.
9. She _____ (taste) _____ the soup, but the preacher did.
10. We are not going home now, but they _____ (be) _____.
11. The baby _____ (cry) _____, but her mother is not.
12. He finished the lesson, but I _____ (do) _____.

13. The rabbit _____ (stick) _____ in the tar, but the bear did not.
14. Boys yell when they play, but girls _____ (do) _____.
15. The meat is cooking, but the potatoes _____ (be) _____.
16. He _____ (chase) _____ the cow, but I did not.
17. The old man _____ (smoke) _____ a pipe, but the boy is not.
18. John lends his pencils, but Bill _____ (do) _____.
19. He _____ (be) _____ clever, but his brother was not.
20. The second girl picked some apples, but the first _____ (do) _____.

Conversation

Answer the following questions, using complete sentences:

1. Where was the preacher when night came?
2. Could he see the moon?
3. Why didn't the preacher sleep at the small house?
4. At the big house, where did he put the horse?
5. What was the first thing he did in the house?
6. How big was the first cat?
7. Which cat was the biggest?
8. What color were the cats' eyes?
9. Did the man see Emmett?
10. Was Emmett afraid?
11. What time will you leave here today?
12. Is there a fireplace in your home?
13. Did you ever see a ghost?
14. When you go to a friend's house, do you usually knock on the door?
15. Is it comfortable to sit on the ground?
16. Are there many clouds today?

Conversation (continued)

17. What does a person do with matches?
18. Do you hesitate before you go outside on a dark night?
19. Is there a fence around the school?
20. What animals usually live in a barn?

Write or Tell

When I Heard a Knock at the Door

How to Make a Fire

Dictation

Listen to, repeat, and then write each of the following sentences:

One dark night a preacher wanted to find a place to sleep. He looked everywhere. At last he decided to stay in a big house alone. He went into the house, but his horse didn't. Inside the house, big black cats began to come from somewhere. The preacher became uncomfortable and left. He had nowhere to go, but he left quickly.

Pronunciation

/ ɚ /	/ hw /
nervous	when
preacher	what
burn	where
heard	why
another	which
first	while

/ ɚ /　The nervous preacher heard the first cat.

/ hw /　Why do you ask where it is when you know?

Unit 2

Little Eight John

Long ago there lived a little boy whose name was Little Eight John. He was a handsome child, but he always did bad things. He was mean. He never did what his mother or father told him to do. He didn't do anything they told him. When someone told him not to do a thing, he went and did it. He didn't care. He liked to make trouble for other people.

"Don't kill insects," his sweet mother told him. "Don't kill insects, or our family will have bad luck. That's the truth."

And Little Eight John said, "No, Mama, I won't kill any

insects. I never will." But then he went into the woods to look for insects.

When he found a fly, he killed it. Sometimes he killed lots of flies. After that, when the cow didn't give milk and Little Eight John's brother had a bad cold, Little Eight John only put his head down and laughed behind his hand.

"Don't sit on the table," his sweet mother told him, "or our family will have lots of trouble."

So Little Eight John sat on every table he saw. When he was able to, he sat on the table at home, and he sat on tables at other people's houses. Then when his mother cut her hand and the wind blew down the chicken house, Little Eight John laughed and laughed and laughed, because he knew why the family had troubles. "I don't care about those old people," he said to himself.

"Don't play games on Sunday," his good father told him, "or it will be bad for the mule."

So Little Eight John, that bad little boy, played games on Sunday after Sunday. Then when his father's mule became sick and couldn't pull the plow, Little Eight John knew why his father had trouble with the mule. He only laughed.

"Don't count your teeth," his dear mother told him, "or there will be a sad sickness in our family."

Little Eight John counted each tooth. He counted his new teeth, and he counted his old teeth. He counted them on weekdays and on weekends. Then his mother got a pain in her back, and his baby sister was very sick. Both almost died. All the troubles were because of that Little Eight John.

"Don't sleep with your head at the foot of the bed, or our family will lose its money," his dear mother told him.

That mean little boy slept with his head at the foot of his bed, and his family lost all its money. Little Eight John only laughed.

"Don't cry on Sundays or the Old Devil Man will get you," his mother told him.

So he cried on Sunday mornings, and he cried on Sunday evenings. He held an onion near his eyes all day Sunday and cried.

In the end the Old Devil Man came for that bad little boy. He changed Little Eight John into a drop of water on the floor. The next day his dear mother cleaned the floor, and the drop of water disappeared.

That was the end of Little Eight John.

Vocabulary

ability	to cry	individual	to refer
able	drop	insect	separately
to blow	fly	onion	trouble
to care	group	pain	wind
to count	handsome	plow	

Idioms

to make trouble	to be able to
to have trouble	to blow down
to care about	the end of
in the end	to refer to

Related Words

end (noun)	pain (noun)	separately (adv.)
to end (verb)	to pain (verb)	separate (adj.)
ending (noun)		to separate (verb)
	plow (noun)	
luck (noun)	to plow (verb)	wind (noun)
lucky (adj.)		windy (adj.)

Opposites

bad—good
end—beginning
handsome—ugly
lucky—unlucky

Structure

I. EACH, ALL, AND BOTH

A. *Each is a singular pronoun. Other pronouns that refer to it must also be in the singular, and the verb used with it must be in the singular form. Each refers to the individual, person or thing thought of separately, in a group of two or more.*

There are twenty of us in this room. **Each** has his book. (If everyone in the room is a girl: **Each** has **her** book.)

B. *All is plural when it refers to count nouns. It refers to the people in a group of three or more, thought of together:*

All of them are sitting with their friends.

All is singular when it refers to mass nouns.

All of the water is gone.

C. *Both is plural. It refers to two people or things, thought of together:*

Bill and John are children. **Both** of them are boys.

D. *Each, all, and both are also often used as adjectives:*

Each girl here has long hair.
All fish live in water.
Both books are on the table.

E. *Complete each of the following sentences by filling in the blanks with each, all, or both:*

1. _____ of us, John and I, are learning English.
2. _____ in the theater like the movie.
3. One pen is black, and the other blue. _____ are good pens.
4. _____ student has his pen.
5. _____ the brother and the sister live in this town.
6. _____ of our neighbors are friendly.
7. _____ works in a different place from the other.
8. _____ neighbor has his house and his garden.
9. Did you give _____ your friend and your brother some soup?
10. Does _____ student want his paper now?
11. Do _____ the students want their papers?
12. The three boys are standing by the door. _____ is wearing his coat.
13. _____ of the three are handsome.
14. The two cats are sitting by the man. _____ of them have big eyes.
15. _____ of his teeth are white.
16. _____ his mother and his father are unhappy.
17. He laughed at _____ his parents.
18. _____ day he disobeyed his mother.
19. She gave _____ boy his supper.
20. _____ the students in school are happy today.

II. CAN AND BE ABLE TO

A. *Can used with another verb shows the ability to do something. Can is generally used for present time. In conversation, the present-tense form is often also used for future time:*

> He **can count** to a hundred.
> He **can do** that work next week.

Structure (continued)

> *The past tense form of <u>can</u> is <u>could</u>:*
>
>> I **could** not **study** last night.
>> **Could** you **see** over their heads?

B. *To show the ability to do something in the future, the phrase <u>will be able to</u> is often used with the main verb. The phrase <u>to be able to</u> also has past- and present-tense forms:*

Past: He **was** not **able to** study yesterday.
Present: Mary **is able to** speak English now.
Future: They **will be able to** go with us to the movies.

C. *Complete each of the following sentences twice: first, using the past or present form of <u>can</u>, and then using the past, present, or future form of <u>to be able to</u>:*

Example: Jim _____ catch the ball yesterday afternoon.
*Jim **could** catch the ball yesterday afternoon.*
*Jim **was able to** catch the ball yesterday afternoon.*

1. I _____ (not) _____ come to class last week.
2. We _____ finish this lesson tomorrow.
3. What languages _____ you speak now?
4. Tom _____ remember the story last week, but now he cannot.
5. I _____ (not) _____ ride a horse.
6. My brother _____ (not) _____ go with us next week.
7. _____ you speak to the class tomorrow?
8. Last Friday I _____ (not) _____ understand this lesson.
9. _____ you understand it now?
10. She _____ (not) _____ milk the cow when it kicked.
11. Sometimes Hans _____ trick other people.
12. _____ you make things disappear?

13. _____ he save lots of money?
14. The thief _____ steal the sheep. No one caught him.
15. The boy _____ (not) _____ smoke a cigarette. He will be sick.

Conversation

Answer the following questions, using complete sentences:

1. Was Little Eight John an ugly little boy?
2. Did he care about his parents?
3. What happened when he sat on the tables?
4. Why did the mule become sick?
5. What did Little Eight John count?
6. Why did the family lose all its money?
7. What did he do to make himself cry?
8. What did the Old Devil Man change the boy into?
9. Why did the drop disappear?
10. Do you think that this story has a sad or happy ending?
11. Do you think that little boys should obey their parents?
12. Can you count to a thousand in English?
13. Is the wind blowing now?
14. Do women here change their names when they marry?
15. Did you ever change your address?
16. Do you have any trouble with English?
17. Are onions good in soup?
18. When a person has a pain, what can he do?
19. Where does a farmer use a plow?
20. Do you like to hear raindrops against the window?

Write or Tell

A Lucky Family

Something I Care About

Dictation

Listen to, repeat, and then write each of the following sentences:

Little Eight John was a handsome little boy, but he did bad things. He didn't care about his parents and he made trouble for them. He made both of them unhappy from the beginning to the end of his life. His mother wasn't able to make him better. In the end, he became a drop of water on the floor.

Pronunciation

/ ə /		/ y /	
handsome	other	yell	year
luck	Sunday	you	yes
Mother	money	yesterday	

/ ə /   Mother gave the other handsome boy money on Sunday.
/ y /   Yes, you yelled yesterday.

Unit 3

Scarface

Once upon a time there was no war. All the Indian people were at peace. In those days there was a man who had a daughter, a very beautiful young girl. Many young men wanted to marry her.

"I do not want a husband," she said.

"Why not?" asked her father. "Some of these young men are rich, handsome, and brave."

"Must I marry already?" she asked. "I am young. I have a rich father and mother. I am used to our home. Why do you worry me?"

The young men held a dance around the campfire. They dressed carefully in their best animal skins, and each one tried to dance better than the others. After they danced, some of them asked the girl to marry them, but she said no to all of them.

Her father was angry. "Why do you say no? All the best young men have asked you."

"Father! Please don't be angry with me. I shall tell you the truth. The Sun told me that I must not marry. The Sun said that I must do what he tells me to do."

"Ah!" said her father. "We must always obey the Sun." They talked no more about it.

There was also a young man who was very poor. His father, mother, and all of his relatives had gone to the Sand Hills.[1] He had no tent, and no wife to make his clothes. He was a handsome young man, but on his face he had a long scar, and his clothes were always old and poor.

After the young men had danced, some of them met Scarface. They laughed at him. "Have you asked the beautiful girl to marry you?" they asked, smiling. "You are rich and handsome."

Scarface said seriously, "I shall do it. I shall go and ask her."

All the other young men laughed and laughed.

Scarface went down to the river. He waited there until the women came to get water, and after a time the girl came, too. "Please," he said, "wait. I want to speak to you. You look so beautiful as you stand there in the sun."

She looked at him carefully.

"You do not want to marry one of those who are handsome and rich and brave. I am poor, and I have an ugly scar on my face. I have no tent, no food, no nice clothes. I have no relatives: all have gone to the Sand Hills. But I must ask you this question. Will you be my wife?"

---

[1] The Sand Hills is a name for the place where Indians believe the soul lives after death.

The girl thought, and soon she said, "True, I do not want to marry one of those rich young men. Now a poor one asks me, and I am glad. You are poor because you have no family. My family is very large. My father can give you dogs. My mother can sew skins together to make us a tent. My people can give us clothes."

The young man was happy in his heart and wanted to kiss her, but she said, "Wait! The Sun has spoken to me. He says I may not marry yet. You must go to the Sun and tell him that you want me for your wife. Ask him to take the scar from your face so that I will know you have seen him."

"Oh!" cried the young man. "At first your words made me happy, but now my heart is sad. Where is the Sun? Where is the path to his tent?"

"You must find him yourself," said the girl. "Be brave." And she left him.

Scarface sat down and covered his head with his hands while he thought about what to do. Then he got up and left the camp of his people.

"Help me, O Sun," he prayed as he walked.

For many days he traveled along rivers and over mountains. He ate only berries and roots.

One day he found a beautiful bow and some arrows on his path, but he did not touch them. He walked carefully around them and traveled farther. Then he met a young man, the handsomest person he had ever seen. The hair of the other young man was long, and his clothes were made of fine skins. The stranger asked, "Did you see my bow and arrows on the path?"

"Yes," said Scarface. "I saw them."

"But you did not touch them?" asked the young man.

"No. I thought someone had left them there, so I did not take them."

"You are not a thief. That is good," said the young man. "What is your name?"

"Scarface."

"Where are you going?"

"To visit the Sun."

"My name is Morning Star," said the young man, "and the Sun is my father. Come with me. I'll take you to our tent."

Soon they came to the Sun's tent. It was very large, and there were beautiful pictures of strange animals on it. Morning Star said, "Do not be afraid, my friend."

They went in. Someone was sitting inside the tent. It was the Moon, Morning Star's mother. She gave Scarface something to eat. "Why have you come so far from your people?" she asked.

"I want to marry the most beautiful girl in the land. I have come to ask the Sun for her," answered Scarface.

Then the Sun returned home. At the doorway he stopped and said, "I smell a person."

"Yes, Father," said Morning Star. "A good young man has come to see you. I know he is good because he found my beautiful bow and arrows on the path and did not touch them."

The Sun came in and sat down. "Tell me now, what can I do for you?" he asked.

"I am here to ask you for the hand of the most beautiful girl in the land," said Scarface. "Please help me. I asked her to marry me, and she was glad, but she told me that she belongs to you."

"Then I'll give her to you. She is yours," said the Sun. "I know that she's a good woman, and the Sun helps good women. They and their husbands and children live a long time."

The Sun put a strong medicine on the young man's face, and the scar disappeared.

Before Scarface returned home, the Moon gave him some fine clothes. She cried and kissed him, and called him, "My son." Morning Star showed him a short path to take to his home.

The young men were surprised when Scarface returned to the camp. He was clothed in fine skins and carried a wonderful bow and some arrows from Morning Star. Some of the young men shouted, "Poor Scarface is here again. But he is not poor now."

All the people ran out of their tents to see him. "Where did you go?" they asked. "Where did you get those beautiful things?"

He did not answer them. In the crowd stood the beautiful young woman. He said to her, "The path was very long, but I found the Sun."

She saw that the scar was gone from his face.

"The Sun said that you may be my wife. He is glad," he said.

And so they were married, and the Sun gave them a long life. They were never sick. When they were very old, one morning their children said, "Wake up! Get up and eat." But they did not answer. In the night their souls had quietly gone to the Sand Hills.

Vocabulary

to accept	camp	to pray	to smile
already	campfire	relative	tent
arrow	to kiss	rich	usual
berry	medicine	root	war
bow	path	sand	yet
brave	peace	scar	

Idioms

in those days   at peace
to talk about   to be used to
to be angry with

Related Words

brave (adj.)	peace (noun)	to pray (verb)
bravely (adv.)	peaceful (adj.)	prayer (noun)
bravery (noun)	peacefully (adv.)	
		to smile (verb)
to kiss (verb)		smile (noun)
kiss (noun)		

Opposites

a brave man—a coward
peace—war
rich—poor
to smile—to frown
in those days—in these days

Structure

I. THE ADVERBS ALREADY AND YET

A. *Already may be used in an affirmative statement, and in either an affirmative or a negative question. It usually precedes the main verb, but it may also be placed at the end of a sentence. The use of already shows that an action has taken place at a time earlier than the time of the statement:*

He is **already** sitting in the classroom.
Haven't we **already** studied this page?
Have you eaten lunch **already**?

B. *Yet is used in negative statements, and in affirmative and negative questions. It is usually placed at the end of a sentence. Yet shows that the action takes place later than the time of the statement, especially in a negative question:*

The teacher isn't here **yet**.
Have you seen that movie **yet**?
Haven't you finished the exercise **yet**?

C. *Use already or yet in each of the following sentences:*

1. Have you _____ read the book?
2. No, I haven't _____.
3. I haven't read the first hundred pages _____.
4. May I go to lunch with you? Have you eaten _____?

5. I'm sorry. I've gone to lunch _____.
6. Has he seen the girls _____?
7. No, not _____.
8. Do you _____ understand these words?
9. Isn't he here _____?
10. Are you finished with the exercise _____? You just began.
11. No, I haven't finished it _____.
12. Is your father home _____?
13. Yes, he is _____ home.
14. Has it stopped raining _____? I expected it to rain all day.
15. Has it stopped raining _____? When it stops, I want to go shopping.

II. TO BE USED TO

A. *To be used to means to accept as usual. It is followed by a noun or noun substitute. Read the following examples:*

I **am used** to this class now.
Are you **used to** your new pen yet?
He has a new baby brother. He **isn't used to** him yet.
They **are used to** walking. They are not tired.

B. *Use the correct form of* to be used to *in each of the following sentences:*

Example: He _____ speaking English.
        *He **is used to** speaking English.*

1. My home is in the country. I _____ (not) _____ living in the city.
2. He _____ pushing his car up the hill.
3. _____ you _____ your new shoes?
4. The new husband _____ (not) _____ his wife's cooking.
5. _____ the little boy _____ tying his own shoes?
6. _____ they _____ the new book yet?
7. _____ the boys _____ peeling potatoes?

Structure (continued)

8. _____ the dog _____ its new home?
9. We usually eat rice. We _____ (not) _____ eating potatoes.
10. I _____ this desk. I don't want another one.

Conversation

Answer the questions, using complete sentences:

1. Why didn't the girl want to marry?
2. Did anyone want to marry her?
3. Who was Scarface?
4. Who told the girl that she should not marry?
5. Why did Scarface go to look for the Sun?
6. What did he eat while he traveled?
7. What did he find on a path?
8. Who was Morning Star?
9. Why did the Sun help Scarface?
10. Did Scarface die young?
11. Do you have many relatives?
12. Do you know the name of a very rich person?
13. When a person is sick what must he have to help him?
14. Does a person usually smile when he is sad?
15. Do you know how to shoot arrows from a bow?
16. Do you think that many people use bows and arrows today?
17. What kind of berries grow here?
18. Is it easier to get up from a chair or from the floor?
19. Where can we find sand?
20. Can you name a root vegetable?

Write or Tell

A Brave Man

My Relatives

Dictation

Listen to, repeat, and then write each of the following sentences:

In a peaceful Indian camp there lived a beautiful girl. Many rich and handsome young men wanted to marry her. "Will you be my wife?" asked a poor man with a scar on his face. "Not yet," said the girl. "First you must ask the Sun." "Oh!" said the unhappy young man. "No one else has visited the Sun. No one knows the way to his tent."

Pronunciation

/ ɚ /	/ ə /	/ f /	/ v /
were	some	face	brave
better	young	careful	wives
heard	along	wife	river
first	run	after	cover
her	husband	food	relative
word	other	father	voice

/ ɚ /	Her first words were better.
/ ə /	Some other young husbands run.
/ ɚ, ə /	Were some young husbands better than others?
/ f /	After eating the food she faced her father.
/ v /	The brave wives heard the voice by the river.
/ f, v /	The wives by the river are careful of food.

Unit 4

Young Melvin

Young Melvin lived on a farm in the country. When his father died, the boy decided to visit the city. He put on his only pair of shoes and called to Bug, his dog. Together they started down the road.

After a short time they came to a neighbor's house, and Melvin knocked on the door.

Old Man Blowdy came to the door and asked, "Who's there?"

"It's Melvin, and Bug, my dog."

Old Man Blowdy opened the door and looked at them. Mr.

Blowdy was not a good man, and he thought that other people were as bad as he was himself.

"What do you want?" he asked.

"I'm going to the city, Mr. Blowdy," said Melvin. "The city is fifty miles away, but I want to go there. I want to see the stores and the lights on the streets. So I've come here first to ask you for your help."

Mr. Blowdy began to close his door. "Now, Melvin, I don't have any money to give you," he said.

"I don't want any money," said Melvin.

Slowly Mr. Blowdy opened the door again. "What do you want, then?"

"I want you to keep my dog, Bug. My father is dead, so he can't keep him."

"Food for a dog costs money, boy," said Old Man Blowdy.

"I'll pay for his food when I come back here to get him," said Melvin.

Mr. Blowdy thought about it. Bug was a handsome young dog. Perhaps he could sell him. The boy Melvin was not intelligent. Everyone knew that. He was honest, but he was simple.

"All right," he said, "I'll keep Bug for you. I'll be glad to do it since you're my neighbor."

So Melvin said good-bye and left his dog with Old Man Blowdy. "I'll come back next week or next year. I don't know when I'll come back because it's fifty miles to the city and fifty miles back."

Weeks passed. Then one day Melvin came back. He went straight to Old Man Blowdy's house and knocked on the door.

"Who's there?" asked Mr. Blowdy from the other side of the door.

"It's Melvin."

"How are you, boy?" Old Man Blowdy asked, slowly opening the door.

"I'm all right. I walked as far as the city and saw everything there. Then I walked back here. I don't want to travel any more until I have a mule to ride."

"That's nice. I'm glad to hear that you had a good time," said Mr. Blowdy.

"Now I want my dog. How much do I owe you for his food?" asked Melvin.

"You owe me five dollars," said the man.

"I have only seventy-five cents. You can have that, and I'll pay you the other four dollars and twenty-five cents later. I didn't think food for a dog was so expensive."

"When can you pay the four dollars and twenty-five cents, boy?"

Melvin hesitated. "Well, I have to wait until I sell my corn. Perhaps I'll have the money then."

"That's a long time, boy, but I'll wait for it," said Old Man Blowdy. He began to close the door, but Melvin had his foot in it.

"Wait a minute! Where is my dog?"

"Bug? I almost forgot. I'm sorry to have to tell you, but your dog died."

"Bug died? How did he die?"

"Well, I put him in the yard to sleep. One night there were so many mosquitoes that they ate him up. The next morning I saw only bones."

Of course, Bug was alive, but Old Man Blowdy wanted to keep him.

Melvin, whose best friend was his dog, had tears in his eyes. "I loved that dog," he said.

He walked as far as Old Man Blowdy's fence. Then he turned around and asked, "May I borrow your mule to ride home? I'm sad and tired now, and I don't want to walk. I'll bring him back to you in the morning."

Old Man Blowdy didn't want to lend his mule, but he wanted Melvin to go away. He didn't want him to hear Bug bark. Since

Melvin was honest, he finally lent him his mule, and the boy rode away.

But the next day Melvin didn't return the mule, and the man began to worry. In the afternoon he walked over to Melvin's house.

"Boy, why haven't you brought me my mule?" he asked.

"I couldn't because yesterday your mule grew wings and flew away," said Melvin, looking at the sky. "I'm very sorry, Mr. Blowdy."

"But mules can't grow wings," Mr. Blowdy said.

"Mosquitoes can't eat up a big dog, either."

Now Old Man Blowdy knew that Melvin wasn't so very stupid. He returned Bug to his owner and forgot about the four dollars and twenty-five cents. Melvin returned the mule.

Vocabulary

alive	to fly	to lend	stupid
to bark	greedy	mosquito	tear
to borrow	to grow	to return (things)	until
to bring	intelligent	sky	wing
distance			especially

Idioms

to eat up	to go straight to
to put on	to bring back
to forget about	as far as
to be glad to	

Related Words

alive (adj.)	greedy (adj.)	intelligent (adj.)
live (adj.)	greedily (adv.)	intelligence (noun)
to live (verb)	greed (noun)	

Opposites

alive—dead
bright—stupid
to bring—to take
greedy—generous
hard—easy
honest—dishonest
intelligent—unintelligent
to lend—to borrow
simple—complicated

Structure

I. ADVERBIAL CLAUSES OF REASON: <u>WHY?</u> . . . <u>BE-CAUSE</u>; <u>SINCE</u>

A. *Clauses answering the question "Why?" are most often introduced by either <u>because</u> or <u>since</u>. Since may be used especially when the question "Why?" is understood and not asked.*

Why are you late? I'm late **because** my watch is slow.
[Why didn't he buy the radio?] He didn't buy the radio **since** it was so expensive.

Clauses beginning with <u>because</u> or <u>since</u> are sometimes placed at the beginning of the sentence:

Because it is cold, we are wearing sweaters.
Since I am sick, I am going to bed.

B. *Answer the questions in parentheses with clauses beginning with <u>since</u>; answer the other questions with clauses beginning with <u>because</u>:*

Example: (*Why is the door open?*)
*The door is open **since** it is so hot in the room.*
*Or, **Since** it is so hot in the room, the door is open.*

1. Why did Melvin go to the city?
2. Why is the light on?
3. (Why did you bring your book to class?)
4. (Why do we sometimes wear raincoats?)
5. (Why do you want to see that movie?)
6. Why is the dog barking?
7. (Why did you give him the book?)
8. (Why did you go shopping yesterday?)
9. Why are you writing that exercise?
10. Why was the mule on the street?
11. (Why can't mules fly?)
12. Why does he know all the answers?
13. Why are his eyes closed?
14. (Why don't you know the time?)
15. (Why did the bell ring?)

II. THE RELATIVE ADJECTIVE <u>WHOSE</u>

A. *<u>Whose</u> refers to a subject or object in the main clause and modifies either the subject or the object of the clause it is in.*

Read these sentences:

The teacher, **whose** book is on the desk, is in the other room.

The boy, **whose** dog is on the farm, is in the city.

He is the boy **whose** father died.

She is the student **whose** paper I forgot.

B. *Put a clause beginning with <u>whose</u> into each of the following sentences:*

Example: The man, _____, visited the school.
*The man, **whose brother is a teacher**, visited the school.*

1. Mrs. Simpson, _____, cleaned the floor.
2. The President, _____, is speaking on the radio.
3. Little Eight John, _____, disobeyed his mother.
4. His mother is the one _____.

Structure (continued)

5. They are the students _____.
6. Mary, _____, is a good cook.
7. The old woman, _____, ate dry bread.
8. He is the old man _____.
9. We are the ones _____.
10. The one, _____, may get this paper after class.

III. UNTIL AND AS FAR AS CONNECTING ADVERBIAL PHRASES AND CLAUSES

A. *Until refers to time, and as far as to distance.*
   Read these sentences:

We worked **until** six o'clock yesterday.
I shall wait **until** you finish your work.
We walked **as far as** the second street.
He did not run **as far as** his brother ran.

B. *Use until or as far as in each of the following sentences:*

1. I can see _____ the river from this window.
2. He will stay with us _____ tomorrow.
3. Melvin went _____ the city.
4. He has bad eyes. He cannot see _____ we can.
5. We will not leave _____ the teacher does.
6. He will not pay the money _____ the storekeeper gives him the oranges.
7. There are mountains _____ you can see.
8. He cannot leave _____ the work is finished.
9. Come with us _____ the park.
10. He fished _____ he caught three fish.
11. I cannot come again _____ next Thursday.
12. This bus will go _____ the next street.
13. The children may play _____ it becomes dark.
14. I can't bring your pencil back _____ this afternoon.
15. Please wait _____ it stops raining.

Conversation

Answer the following questions, using complete sentences:

1. What was the dog's name in the story?
2. Who was Old Man Blowdy?
3. What did Melvin want to see in the city?
4. How far away was the city?
5. How much money did Melvin owe Mr. Blowdy?
6. How much money did he have?
7. What did Melvin borrow?
8. Had mosquitoes eaten up Melvin's dog?
9. Was Mr. Blowdy honest?
10. When Melvin returned the mule, what did Old Man Blowdy forget about?
11. When are there many mosquitoes?
12. Did you bring two pencils to school today?
13. Do greedy people like to give things away?
14. When do dogs like to bark?
15. Do honest people usually return what they borrow?
16. Are dogs as intelligent as people?
17. Was this lesson simple?
18. Is your great-grandfather still alive?
19. What do birds need to fly?
20. What grows around the school?

Write or Tell

Dogs

Mosquitoes

Dictation

Listen to, repeat, and then write each of the following sentences:

Because his father had died, Melvin did not have to stay at home. He decided to put on his shoes and walk as far as the city. He left his dog with his neighbor, whose name was Old Man Blowdy. Since he was greedy, he did not want to return the dog when Melvin came back. But Melvin was intelligent. He kept the mule until Mr. Blowdy gave back his dog.

Pronunciation

/ aɪ /	/ ʃ /
I	finish
died	shall
time	should
light	sunshine
mile	she
five	show
tired	

/ aɪ /   After five miles, I was tired.
/ ʃ /   She shall show us the sunshine.

Unit 5

The Judge

One day a rattlesnake lay in the sun. He lay at the bottom of a mountain. The sun was warm, and he went to sleep. Suddenly a big stone fell down the mountain. It fell on top of the rattlesnake, so that he woke up and found he could not move.

The rattlesnake lay under the stone for many hours. He was afraid that no one was going to come by and help him. He tried to move, but the stone lay across his back and kept him a prisoner.

Finally a rabbit came around the mountain. He was happy as he went through the grass in the warm sunshine. Then he saw the snake under the stone and stopped to speak to him.

"Good morning, Mr. Rattlesnake," said the rabbit. "Do you enjoy sitting under that stone?"

"Don't tease me!" said the angry snake. "The stone hurts me very much. Move it off me, and I shall give you a reward."

The rabbit knew that the snake was unfriendly and dangerous, but he was kindhearted. He didn't like to see other animals in pain, so he went slowly toward the stone.

"All right, I'll move it," the rabbit said.

He tried to pick the stone up, but it was too heavy. First he pushed on one side, and then he pushed on the other. At last he pushed the heavy stone off the rattlesnake. The snake was free, and the rabbit was very tired.

"Now I shall give you your reward," said the rattlesnake.

"Oh, no, thank you," said the rabbit. "I don't want a reward. I would just like to go home now. You should move out of the sun, too."

"It is a nice reward," the snake said.

"What is it?" asked the rabbit.

"You helped me," said the snake, "so now I am going to eat you for my dinner."

"No! No!" cried the rabbit. "That is not a reward. Please do not eat me, Mr. Snake. I'm too tired to run away from you."

"Yes, yes," said the rattlesnake. His eyes followed the rabbit, and he moved slowly toward him. "I must have my dinner."

Just then a coyote came around the mountain.

"What is happening here?" the coyote asked.

Both the rabbit and the snake began to talk at the same time. "You can be our judge," they said.

"What happened?" asked the coyote.

"I came here and found Mr. Rattlesnake under this stone," the rabbit said. "He couldn't move, so I pushed the stone off him. He said he wanted to give me a reward. I don't want a reward, but I want my life! Now he wants to eat me! He says that is my reward."

"That is not the truth," the snake said. "I was under the stone. That is true. But I always sleep under a stone. I don't like the hot sun. Mr. Rabbit pushed the stone and tried to kill me. Now I want to eat him for punishment."

The coyote put his chin in his hand and looked at both the rabbit and the snake. Then he said slowly, "My friends, you agree that Mr. Snake was under the stone, don't you?"

"Yes," said the rabbit. "That is true."

"Yes," said the snake. "That is true."

"Well," said the coyote, "I must see you as you were, Mr. Rattlesnake. Please lie by the stone again. Mr. Rabbit and I will put it on top of you. Then I'll understand who is telling the truth."

The snake agreed. The rabbit and the coyote put the stone on top of him.

"Now," said the coyote. "Is this how you were?"

"Yes," said the rattlesnake. "This is how I was."

"Can you move?" asked the coyote.

The snake tried, but he couldn't move.

"Then you must stay under the stone, and Mr. Rabbit can go home to his family."

Vocabulary

to agree	to hurt	prisoner	snake
bottom	judge	to push	to tease
chin	kind	rattlesnake	unfriendly
dangerous	mountain	reward	would

Idioms

to be in pain	kind-hearted
on top of	out of
at the same time	would like

Related Words

agreeable (adj.)	judge (noun)	kind (adj.)
to agree (verb)	to judge (verb)	kindness (noun)
agreement (noun)	judgment (noun)	
		reward (noun)
dangerous (adj.)		to reward (verb)
danger (noun)		
dangerously (adv.)		

Opposites

to agree—to disagree
bottom—top
dangerous—safe
kind—unkind
reward—punishment
unfriendly—friendly

Structure

I. PRACTICE WITH THE PREPOSITIONS ACROSS, AROUND, TOWARD, UP, INTO, THROUGH, OUT OF, DOWN

A. *Read these sentences after your teacher:*

He went **across** the street.
He went **toward** the house.
He went **around** the house.
He went **up** the steps.
He went **into** the house.
He went **through** the house.
He went **out of** the house.
He went **down** the steps.

B. *Use one of the prepositions listed above in each of the following blanks:*

1. I walked _____ the tree three times.
2. The cat climbed _____ the tree, but it was afraid to climb _____.
3. The sun goes _____ in the west.
4. Who is sitting _____ the room from you?
5. Is he putting sugar _____ his coffee?
6. The boy put his hand _____ when he wanted to speak.
7. Please take your book _____ your desk.
8. The ball went _____ the window, but it didn't hit it.
9. My finger is too large. The ring will not go _____ it.
10. The bone fell _____ the dog's mouth.
11. We cannot see _____ that dirty window.
12. The cloud moved _____ the moon.
13. Do you want to go _____ in an airplane?
14. We walked _____ the park and then went home.
15. He lives _____ the street from the school.

II. WOULD LIKE

A. *Would like means want, but it is more polite. Would is used with the simple form of the main verb like for present or future time:*

I **would like** some water. **Would** you **like** some, too?
(I **want** some water. **Do** you **want** some, too?)
Would you **like** to have this red pencil?
I **would like** to visit you tomorrow. Thank you for the invitation.

Would is followed by have and the past participle of like for past time:

I **would have liked** to visit you yesterday.
He **would have liked** to see the movie we saw.
His sister **would** not **have liked** it.

Structure (continued)

> **B.** *Use the correct form of* <u>*would like*</u> *to replace* <u>*want*</u> *in each of the following sentences.*
>
> *Example: He **wants** to borrow a pencil.*
> *He **would like** to borrow a pencil.*

1. **Do** you **want** to climb the mountain with us?
2. No, I **don't want** to climb the mountain.
3. He **wanted** to see the movie, but we went without him.
4. **Doesn't** he **want** to study?
5. Yes, he **wants** to study, but he needs another book.
6. What **do** you **want** to do now?
7. I **want** to take a walk.
8. I don't think they **want** to go with us.
9. When you **want** another piece of paper, please tell me.
10. **Didn't** they **want** to see the football game?

Conversation

Answer the following questions, using complete sentences:

1. Where was the rattlesnake sleeping?
2. Where did the stone fall from?
3. Was the rabbit unfriendly?
4. What did the rabbit do for the snake?
5. What did the snake want to do to the rabbit?
6. Who was the judge?
7. Did the snake tell the truth?
8. Did the rabbit try to kill the snake?
9. Where is the rattlesnake now?
10. Do you think that the coyote was a good judge? Why or why not?
11. Is it hard to push a car?
12. Is it dangerous to tease rattlesnakes?
13. What is at the bottom of the blackboard?

14. For what may a person receive an award?
15. Do you try to be kind to animals?
16. Where is a person's chin?
17. The sun is warm today. Do you agree?
18. Is it easy to hurt yourself with a knife?
19. Can you listen to the radio and read at the same time?
20. What is on top of this school?

Write or Tell

A Dangerous Animal

A Kindhearted Person I Know

Dictation

Listen to, repeat, and then write each of the following sentences:

Rattlesnakes are dangerous and unfriendly animals. I would not like to pick one up. Most people are afraid of rattlesnakes, but at the same time most rattlesnakes are afraid of people. When people come toward them, they move quickly away. They can hurt you when you step on top of them.

Pronunciation

/ æ /	/ a /	/ dʒ /
rabbit	lots	judge
rattlesnake	not	job
and	want	jump
animal	are	just
happen	job	

/ æ /	Rabbits and rattlesnakes are animals.
/ a /	Lots of us do not want a job.
/ æ, a /	Rabbits and other animals do not want lots.
/ dʒ /	"I just jump," said the judge.

Unit 6

Jim and the Angel

There was a farmer named Jim who prayed every night before he went to bed. "I don't want to stay here," he said. "I want an angel to come and take me to heaven. I'm lonely. I'm unhappy. I have to work too hard. I'm tired. I want an angel to take me off this earth. I want to go to heaven soon."

One night a friend passed Jim's house and heard him praying. He stopped and listened to his words through the open window. Then he went home and got a white bed sheet which he put over his head. After that, he returned to Jim's house.

Jim heard someone outside his door. He stopped praying and asked, "Who's that?"

His friend said from under the sheet, "I'm an angel, Jim. I've come to take you to heaven."

"Tell the angel that I'm not here, Jane," Jim told his wife. He got under the bed.

At first Jane didn't say anything, but the voice outside the door said, "Come on, Jim. Come go with me to heaven now. You can stop working. You can stop worrying. Come on, Jim."

Jane said, "Jim isn't here, angel. Come back another time."

The voice said, "Then *you* come with me, Jane. I will take you, instead."

"Jim, come out from under the bed and go with the angel," Jane whispered. "You asked him to come for you. Now go with him."

Jim without saying a word, continued to lie under the bed, and the voice outside called again, "Come on, Jane."

Jane said to Jim, "I thought you wanted to go to heaven. Come out and go with the angel."

Jim whispered, "Didn't you hear the angel call, 'Come on, Jane'? You go with him."

"I'm not going to go anywhere. You asked him to come, and I'm going to tell him that you're here."

Outside the man under the sheet said, "Come on, Jane."

"Oh, angel, Jim is here under the bed," Jane said.

"Come on, then, Jim," the voice said. "Come and go to heaven with me."

Slowly, Jim came out from under the bed. He went to the door and looked into the darkness outside. There he saw a big white thing. He said, "Oh, angel, I can't go to heaven in these old pants. Please let me put on my best pants."

"All right, Jim. Put on your best pants."

Jim took a long time to change his pants, but when he again went to the door, the white thing was still outside. He said, "Oh, angel, please let me put on my best shirt."

"All right, Jim. Go and put on your best shirt."

Jim took a long time to put on his best shirt, but when he returned to the door, the angel was still there. He said, "Angel, I'm ready to go with you, but I'm a poor ugly man. I can't come very near to you. Please move back a little."

His friend in the sheet moved back a short way.

"Oh, angel," Jim said, "you know that you are greater than I. I can't come near to you. Please step farther back."

The friend stepped back a few more steps.

"Angel," Jim said, "you're so strong and I'm so weak. Please step back some more."

His friend lifted his foot to take another step, and Jim ran out of the door like lightning. He ran through the dark fields, and his friend with the white sheet ran after him.

Three days later Jim came home. He was tired and sat down in a chair by his wife.

"Do you want to stay here on earth now?" asked Jane.

"I think so," said Jim. "It's a good place to live if you like it, and a good place to die if you don't. I'm one man who likes it."

Vocabulary

angel	lightning	sheet
conditional	lonely	ugly
darkness	outside	weak
great	poor	to whisper
heaven	to return	

Idioms

to get under	out from under
to go on	to move (or step) back
to come out	

Related Words

great (adj.)	poor (adj.)	weak (adj.)
greatness (noun)	poorly (adv.)	weakly (adv.)
	poor (noun)	

Opposites

outside—inside
poor—rich (or good)
to return—to go away, to leave
ugly—pretty, handsome
weak—strong
to whisper—to yell

Structure

I. CONDITIONAL CLAUSES WITH <u>IF</u>

A. *A clause introduced by* <u>if</u> *is called conditional and is always connected to a main clause. The main clause shows the result of the condition described in the secondary clause. The present tense is used in the* <u>if</u> *clause for both future and present possibility.*

If it rains, I will not go swimming.
If he wants to, he may come in.
If you want that book, you must go to the library.

The conditional clause may also follow the main clause:

I don't want the apple **if it isn't good.**
Please buy me some candy **if you go to the store.**

B. *Use the proper form of the verb in parentheses in each of the following sentences:*

Structure (continued)

> *Example: If he* _____ (*visit*) _____ *us next week, I want to show him our garden.*
>
> *If he visits us next week, I want to show him our garden.*

1. We can have class outside if the weather _____ (be) _____ good.
2. If he _____ (ask) _____ a question, the teacher will answer it.
3. If you _____ (be) _____ finished, we can go now.
4. We will listen if he _____ (speak) _____.
5. If you _____ (not run) _____, you will be late.
6. If it _____ (rain) _____ tomorrow, we can't go for a walk.
7. If we _____ (study) _____, we can learn a lot of English.
8. I want to stay inside if there _____ (be) _____ lightning.
9. If the old man _____ (eat) _____ too much, he will be sick.
10. I shall go if John _____ (go) _____ too.

C. Answer the following questions, using an _if_ clause in your answer:

> *Example: What will you do if it rains this afternoon?*
> *I'll stay inside if it rains.*

1. If a person is sick, what should he do?
2. If you lose your pencil, what will you do?
3. Will you visit us this evening if you have time?
4. Will you tell me if you go to the movies?
5. What must you do if you want a new shirt?
6. If I see some chalk, shall I buy you some?
7. If the policeman catches the thief, what will he do?
8. What will we see if we go to the country?
9. What will happen if you forget your book?
10. If you wake up in the night, do you go back to sleep?

II. SO AS A CLAUSE SUBSTITUTE

A. *So is often used in spoken English as a substitute for a noun clause introduced by that. It follows such verbs as say, tell, think, and believe. It is usually used in an answer to a question:*

Are you finished?
   I think **so.** [I think **that I am finished.**]
Is he going to go with us?
   I don't know. He didn't say **so.** [He didn't say **that he was going with us.**]

B. *Answer the following questions, using so as a clause substitute.*

   Example: Who told you that John is sick?
            His mother told me so.

   1. Do you believe that this is the last lesson in the book?
   2. Who said that we should open our books?
   3. Do you think that Jim wanted to go to heaven?
   4. Do books tell us that the earth is round?
   5. Do your friends believe that you know a lot of English?
   6. Do they think that you are a good student?
   7. Who knows that New York is in the United States?
   8. Did you say that you live near here?
   9. Do you believe that it rained this morning?
   10. Do you think that these questions are difficult?
   11. Who told us that we could study in this room?
   12. Did Jim say that he wanted to work hard?
   13. Did he believe that there was an angel in his yard?
   14. Did you say that you forgot your notebook?
   15. Who said that you forgot it?

Conversation

Answer the following questions, using complete sentences:

1. What did Jim do every night?
2. Who heard him speaking?
3. What did his friend put over his head?
4. What did he pretend that he was?
5. Where did Jim hide?
6. Did Jane want to go with the angel?
7. What color was the bed sheet?
8. Why did the angel have to wait a long time?
9. Could Jim run very fast?
10. When did Jim come home?
11. Do you like to see lightning?
12. Do people often whisper in a library?
13. Can a weak person lift heavy things?
14. Do you prefer to be outside or inside in the darkness?
15. Does it take a long time to eat breakfast?
16. Is a person always lonely when he is alone?
17. When will you return home today?
18. Does a man usually need a long time to change his shirt?
19. When you see a snake, do you step back?
20. Do poor people usually have to work hard?

Write or Tell

A Place to Whisper

When There Is Lightning

Dictation

Listen to, repeat, and then write each of the following sentences:

Jim thought that he wanted to die, but his friend didn't think so. He put a sheet over his head and stood outside Jim's door. "If you want to go to heaven, come with me," he said. When Jim thought about it, he knew that he wanted to stay on the earth. "The earth is a good place to live if you like it," he said.

Pronunciation

/ ɔɪ /	/ tʃ /
noise	question
voice	much
boy	chair
point	picture

/ ɔɪ /   We heard the noisy boy's voice.
/ tʃ /   The question is, "Is the chair near the picture?"

Unit 7

The Talking Eggs

Once there was a bad woman who had two daughters. Their names were Rose and Blanche. Rose was also bad, but Blanche was good. The mother liked Rose better, because she understood her. She made Blanche do all the work while Rose sat in a chair all day.

One day the mother sent Blanche to the well to get some water. Blanche had taken water from the well when an old woman came to her.

"Please give me some water," the old woman said. "I'm thirsty."

"Yes, aunt," Blanche said. "Here is some water."

"Thank you, my child," the old woman said. "Now I'm not thirsty any longer. You are a good girl."

A few days later the mother was angry about something. She hit Blanche with the broom and said, "Go away. I don't want to see you any more."

Blanche was afraid of her mother, and she ran into the woods. She cried because she didn't know where to go. Then she met the same old woman that she had seen at the well.

"My child, why have you been crying?" the old woman asked.

"Oh, aunt," Blanche said, "Mama beat me and told me not to come home any more, but I don't know where to go."

"Come with me, my child. I'll give you supper and a bed to sleep in. But you have to promise not to laugh at anything."

The old woman took Blanche's hand, and they began to walk through the woods. After a time Blanche saw two arms. The arms were fighting. She thought that was strange, but she said nothing, and she did not laugh. Later she saw two legs fighting, and finally she saw two heads fighting.

"Will you still go with me?" asked the old woman.

"Yes," said Blanche.

At last they arrived at the old woman's home. The old woman said, "Make a fire, my child, to cook the supper." Then she took off her head and sat down. She put her head on her knees and began to comb her white hair. Blanche thought that was very strange, and she was afraid, but she said nothing.

When she had finished combing her hair, the old woman put her head in its place on her neck. She gave Blanche a bone to cook for their supper. When Blanche put the bone into a pan, and the pan on the fire, the pan became full of good meat.

They ate their supper and went to bed.

The next morning the old woman said, "You must go home now, but because you are a good girl, I want to give you a gift. Go to the chicken house and take some eggs. Take the ones that say, 'Take me.' You must not take the ones that say 'Don't take me.' As you walk home, throw the eggs behind your back to break them."

Blanche walked home, throwing the eggs behind her back. Many pretty things came out of the eggs. There were diamonds and pieces of gold and pretty dresses. Blanche picked them all up. Now she had many pretty things of her own, so her mother was very glad to see her.

The next day the mother said to Rose, "You must go to the woods and find the old woman. You must have pretty things, too."

Rose went into the woods and she met the old woman. She agreed to follow her to her home. On the way she saw the arms, the legs, and the heads fighting, and she laughed. The old woman said, "My child, you are not a good girl."

Rose slept in the old woman's house one night. The next morning the old woman said to her, "You must go home now. Go to the chicken house and take only the eggs that say, 'Take me.'"

Rose went to the chicken house and took all the eggs that said, "Don't take me." She put them into her pockets and went away with them.

As she walked home, she broke the eggs. Inside were snakes and frogs and lizards. They began to chase her. Rose ran from them, screaming and yelling. She ran to her mother. And when her mother saw all the creatures chasing Rose, she became frightened and angry. She became so frightened and angry that she sent Rose away. She told her to go and live in the woods by herself.

Vocabulary

certain	to emphasize	gift	plus
to chase	event	knee	pocket
definite	to fight	leg	to promise
diamond	frightened	lizard	

Idioms

to make someone do (something)
to be angry about something
in its place

to ask for
to keep a promise

Related Words

definite (adj.)
definitely (adv.)

to emphasize (verb)
emphasis (noun)

to fight (verb)
fight (noun)

knee (noun)
to kneel (verb)

to promise (verb)
promise (noun)

Opposites

to chase—to run from
to keep a promise—to break a promise

Structure

I. ADVERBS OF TIME: STILL, ANY MORE, ANY LONGER

A. *Still means continuing at this time. It may be used in affirmative and certain negative sentences. In affirmative sentences it is usually placed before a verb of action, but after any form of the verb to be:*

The children **still** play in the yard.
The children are **still** playing in the yard.
He is **still** here.

In negative sentences still is generally placed before the main verb and its auxiliaries:

I **still** do not understand English.
He **still** is not reading the book.

Structure (continued)

> **B.** *Any more is used in negative sentences. It is generally put at the end of the sentence. Any more refers to the time following some earlier time or event:*

> The children didn't play in the yard **any more.**
> He was happy, but he isn't **any more.**
> He isn't reading the book **any more.**

> **C.** *Any longer is used in almost the same way as any more. It emphasizes the time:*

> I don't want to stay here **any longer.**
> You shouldn't wait **any longer.** Go to the doctor.

> **D.** *Use still, any more, or any longer in each of the following sentences:*

>   1. He doesn't want to talk to us _____.
>   2. I _____ don't know your name.
>   3. Please don't wait for me _____.
>   4. The man is _____ in his field.
>   5. Can't he read English _____?
>   6. Are you _____ writing the exercise?
>   7. Let's not study _____. Let's take a walk.
>   8. Don't you like corn _____?
>   9. I _____ have many things to do.
> 10. He isn't going to stay _____, but I am.
> 11. We _____ haven't finished this lesson.
> 12. We are _____ doing the exercises.
> 13. I don't see John _____ because he lives in another city.
> 14. It's eight o'clock. He shouldn't sleep _____.
> 15. He used to live here, but he doesn't _____.

II. PAST AND PRESENT PERFECT WITH -ING

> **A.** *Have (or has) been plus the present participle of a verb may be used to describe an action that was begun in the*

past and is continuing into the present. **The time when the action began is usually given:**

I **have been reading** this book **since yesterday** afternoon. [I am reading it now.]

He **has been sitting** in this classroom **for two hours**. [He is sitting here now.]

B. *Had been plus the present participle of a verb tells of an action that began at some time in the past and continued to some definite stated time or moment:*

I **had been playing** with the children **until I saw him.** [I wasn't playing with them any more. I played with the children before I saw him.]

Yesterday he **had been sleeping** for three hours **when I woke him up.**

[When I woke him up, his sleeping stopped. He slept before I woke him up.]

C. *Complete each of the following sentences, giving the past or the present perfect form of the verb with* -ing *as asked for in the parentheses.*

Example: He _____ (*sit*) _____ *by the tree a long time. (Present perfect)*
He has been sitting by the tree a long time.

1. He _____ (wait) _____ there for three hours when his brother came. (Past)
Is he waiting there now?

2. We _____ (study) _____ this lesson for two days now. (Present)
Are we studying it now?

3. I _____ (not do) _____ my homework since Monday. (Present)
Am I doing it now?

4. _____ he _____ (work) _____ in the garden all day? (Present)
Is he working in the garden now?

Structure (continued)

5. Jane _____ (sing) _____ in the next room since two o'clock. (Present)
   Is she singing now?
6. John _____ (lie) _____ in the sun when we called him. (Past)
   Is he lying in the sun now?
7. She _____ (worry) _____ about her son since he left home. (Present)
   Is she worrying now?
8. We _____ (walk) _____ in the park only two minutes when it began to rain. (Past)
   Are we walking in the park now?
9. The boys _____ (not play) _____ football since school began. (Present)
   Are they playing now?
10. What _____ you _____ (do) _____ since I saw you yesterday? (Present)
   Are you doing it now?

Conversation

Answer the following questions, using complete sentences:

1. Which daughter was like her mother?
2. Who did all the work?
3. Where did Blanche first see the old woman?
4. What did Blanche see that was strange?
5. How long did she stay with the old woman?
6. Where did Blanche find the eggs?
7. Why was her mother glad to see her again?
8. Which eggs did Rose take?
9. Where did she first put the eggs?
10. What began to chase her?
11. Do you think that diamonds are pretty?
12. Are most people afraid of snakes and lizards?

13. When a person has a birthday in your country, does he usually receive gifts?
14. How many legs does a lizard have?
15. Is the teacher's table in the right place?
16. Is it easy to make boys stop fighting?
17. Are your knees under your desk?
18. Is there a pencil in your pocket?
19. Is it better to keep or to break a promise?
20. What is John angry about?

Write or Tell

A Good Person I Know

Something to Be Afraid of

Dictation

Listen to, repeat, and then write each of the following sentences:

Blanche had been doing all the work for her mother before her mother sent her away. After that, she didn't have to work so hard any more. Because she was good, an old woman gave her some magic eggs that had diamonds inside them. Rose, her bad sister, took the eggs that had lizards inside them. Rose is still unhappy, because she doesn't live with her mother any longer.

Pronunciation

/ i /	/ ɪ /	/ dʒ /	/ tʃ /
see	it	judge	child
receive	did	jump	Blanche
me	promise	just	chicken
please	gift	job	chase
meat	chicken		

/ i /	Please give me the meat.
/ ɪ /	Did you promise a gift of chicken?
/ i, ɪ /	I didn't see the pretty gift.
/ dʒ /	The judge just did the job.
/ tʃ /	The child Blanche chased the chicken.
/ dʒ, tʃ /	The child and the judge jumped for the chicken.

Unit 8

The Hunter and the Raven

Once upon a time, there was in an Eskimo village an unhappy
young man. All the men in the village were hunters, and this
young man was a hunter, too. But he could hit nothing with his
arrows. Every day he took his bow and arrows and went hunting,
but he never killed anything. He had to eat the meat that other
men brought home, and he was ashamed.

"Why don't you ever shoot anything?" the men asked. "Are
you afraid?" They laughed at him. "Are you a man or a baby?"

The young man looked at the ground and did not answer.

59

After a time the young man became so unhappy and ashamed that he decided to kill himself. He decided that he would freeze to death in the snow. One cold day he went to a place far from the village. There he took off his warm fur coat and pants, and lay down in the snow.

He waited to die, but for some reason he didn't freeze. His body remained warm, and the snow melted under him. He lay there for a long time with his eyes closed, trying to freeze.

Then, near his head, he heard Mr. and Mrs. Raven speaking.

"Here's a dead man," said Mr. Raven.

"Yes, yes," said Mrs. Raven. "Cut out his eyes."

"But, on second thought, perhaps he isn't dead," said Mr. Raven.

"Oh, yes, he is dead," said Mrs. Raven. "You can see. The foxes have taken his clothes."

"Yes, you are right," said Mr. Raven. "I shall cut out his eyes." So Mr. Raven took his knife and jumped onto the man's nose.

The young man was thinking, "To freeze is one thing, but to lose my eyes is another thing."

"I don't want my eyes cut out!" he shouted and jumped to his feet.

At this, Mr. Raven fell to the ground, and the hunter took his knife. "Come here," said the young man to the two ravens.

"What do you want?" they asked. They remained at a safe distance from the hunter.

"I am a hunter, and I want to kill you, of course," said the young man.

"You are not a very good hunter," said Mr. Raven. "Give me my knife."

"Oh, no," said the young man.

"I shall reward you for my knife. Give it to me, and you will become a great hunter."

"Are you telling the truth?" asked the young man.

"Yes. When you shoot an arrow, you will always hit a caribou or a bear."

"That is good pay for your knife," said the man. "Here it is." He returned the knife to Mr. Raven.

"But remember one thing," said the raven. "Always cut out the eyes of the animal before you skin it."

"I promise that I shall do that," said the young man.

Then the two ravens flew away.

The young man began to feel cold, so he put on his fur coat and his fur pants and went home. The next day he went out of the village to hunt. Soon he saw a caribou and killed it. He cut the eyes out first, and then he began to cut off the hide. While he was working, Mr. and Mrs. Raven flew down and ate the eyes.

Day after day the young man went with his bow and arrows and hunted for caribou. He was always successful. Sometimes the other hunters could not find anything to shoot, but the young man always did.

"You are a great hunter," said the other men. They didn't laugh at him now.

But the young man became too proud of his success. One day he killed a caribou, and he did not cut out the eyes. "I am a great hunter," he said to himself. "Why must I do what I don't want to do? I don't want to cut out the eyes." So he skinned the animal and took it home.

He wandered all the next day, but he saw no animals. The day after, he still found nothing. The third day he saw some caribou, but his arrows flew either in front of them or behind them, and they ran away.

"I don't ever again want to go hunting among people who will laugh at me," he told himself. "I will go away from the village and lie in the snow as I did before."

So the young man went to the place where he had seen Mr. and Mrs. Raven the first time. There he took off his warm fur coat and his warm fur pants, and lay down between them in the snow. But this time he did not remain warm, and the ravens did not fly over him. Soon the young man froze and died.

Vocabulary

caribou	to hunt	raven	success
Eskimo	hunter	to remain	successful
to feel	to melt	to shout	village
to freeze	nose	to skin	to wander
fur	rarely		

Idioms

on second thought

to laugh at

to cut off

to cut out

to be proud of

Related Words

to skin (verb)

skin (noun)

success (noun)

successful (adj.)

successfully (adv.)

Opposites

to freeze—to melt

to remain—to leave, to go away

to shout—to whisper

Structure

I. PRACTICE WITH THE PREPOSITIONS <u>OVER</u>, <u>UNDER</u>, <u>ABOVE</u>, <u>BELOW</u>, <u>BETWEEN</u>, <u>AMONG</u>, <u>IN FRONT OF</u>, AND <u>BEHIND</u>

A. *Read these sentences after your teacher:*

The light is **over** John's head.
My feet are **under** my desk.
The sky is **above** us.
I see lots of trees **below** me.
He is **between** two desks.
He is **among** lots of people.
He is **in front of** the mule.
He shouldn't be **behind** the mule.

B. *Use the right preposition in each of the following blanks. In some sentences more than one preposition may be correct.*

1. There is nothing _____ my desk and yours.
2. We have a ceiling _____ our heads.
3. I can't find it _____ all these papers.
4. From the top of the mountain we saw the village _____.
5. The wall is _____ the picture.
6. _____ the school is the street.
7. We walked _____ the bridge.
8. She put a sheet _____ the bed.
9. Where there are many clouds, airplanes can fly _____ them.
10. _____ the books in the library, did you find one that you like?
11. The book that I was looking for was _____ my nose.
12. If you look out the window, you can see the boys _____ in the garden.
13. Mary is sitting _____ John and Jim.

Structure (continued)

> 14. The clouds are _____ our heads, and the grass
> _____ our feet.
> 15. _____ the teacher's desk is the blackboard.

II. FREQUENCY WORDS WITH <u>ANYTHING</u>, <u>SOMETHING</u>, <u>ANYONE</u>, <u>SOMEONE</u>, ETC.

A. *Something, <u>someone</u>, and <u>somebody</u> (like <u>some</u>) may be used in questions and affirmative statements. They can be used only with affirmative frequency words such as <u>always</u>, <u>often</u>, <u>usually</u>, <u>sometimes</u>, and <u>generally</u>.*

Do you always eat **something** for breakfast?
> Yes, I always do. I always eat **something**.

<u>Anything</u>, <u>anyone</u>, *and* <u>anybody</u> *(like <u>any</u>) are used in questions and negative statements. They are used with negative frequency words, such as <u>never</u>, <u>rarely</u> and <u>seldom</u>.*

Do you know **anyone** in this room?
> No, I have never met **anyone** here.

<u>Nothing</u> *and* <u>no one</u> *(<u>nobody</u>) are themselves negative, and should not be used with the word <u>not</u>. Of the frequency words only <u>ever</u> is used with <u>nothing</u> and <u>no one</u>.*

Does **no one** ever want to study with me?
> No, **no one** ever wants to study with you.
> [No, **not anyone** ever wants to study with him.]

<u>Everything</u> *and* <u>everyone</u> *(<u>everybody</u>) may be used in negative or affirmative statements, negative or affirmative questions, and with all frequency words:*

Do you ever know **everything** in the lesson?
> No, I seldom know **everything**.
> Yes, I often know **everything** in the lesson.

B. *Answer the following questions, first in the affirmative and then in the negative. Use long answers.*

Example: Did he ever shoot anything?
   Yes, he sometimes shot something.
   No, he never shot anything.

1. Do you ever pick up anything when you take a walk?
2. Do you always finish everything that you begin?
3. Do you ever speak to anyone whom you don't know?
4. Does he ever complain about anything?
5. Does someone always open the window in the morning?
6. Does your brother sometimes say something about this class?
7. Has the baby ever cried about anything?
8. Does the teacher ever leave something at home?
9. Has your friend ever met anyone from America?
10. Do you always believe everything that people say?
11. Does the class usually write something?
12. Has a thief ever stolen anything from you?
13. Have those men ever borrowed anything from you?
14. Have you ever seen anyone push a plow?
15. Has no one in the class ever seen a rabbit?

Conversation

Answer the following questions, using complete sentences:

1. Why was the young man unhappy?
2. What did he take with him when he went hunting?
3. Why did he lie down in the snow?
4. Whom did he hear speaking by his head?
5. What did he take away from Mr. Raven?
6. Why did he become a great hunter?
7. What kind of animals did he hunt?
8. Why did he become a bad hunter again?
9. Why did he lie down in the snow a second time?
10. What kind of clothes did he wear?
11. What does one need to shoot an arrow?

Conversation (continued)

12. When does water freeze?
13. Can you remember a story about a rabbit?
14. Do you need fur clothes to keep warm?
15. Are parents usually proud of their children?
16. Have you ever seen a raven?
17. Are there any caribou in your country?
18. When will ice melt quickly?
19. Would you like to go hunting?
20. How long will you remain here today?

Write or Tell

Something to Be Proud of

Winter in My Country

Dictation

Listen to, repeat, and then write each of the following sentences:

When the young man was among the other hunters, he was ashamed because they laughed at him. He could not hit anything. He lay down in the snow to kill himself, but the snow melted under him. After he returned Mr. Raven's knife, he became a great hunter. He became so proud of himself that he didn't care about his promise to Mr. Raven. Then he never shot anything again, and he froze to death in the snow.

Pronunciation

/ yu /	/ s /	/ z /
few	decide	freeze
mule	pants	please
you	soon	eyes
usually	first	nose
use	snow	lose
	see	

/ yu /   You usually see few mules.

/ s /   We'll see the first snow soon.

/ z /   Please don't freeze your nose.

/ s, z /   It will please me to see the first snow freeze soon.

Unit 9

Too Tired to Move

Once there was a family of seven people. The children were the same as their mother and father. They were all lazy. Only the father was somewhat different from his wife and children: he was the laziest of all.

One day these people lay like logs under a tree in their yard, breathing the sweet summer air. They could watch the crows eating the corn in their cornfield, but they were too lazy to go into the sunshine to chase the birds away.

Suddenly, from far away, the family's dog, Rover, began to bark.

"I know that none of us around here wants to move to see what Rover wants," said one, lifting his head from the ground, "but why do you think he is barking?"

"Probably he buried a bone and can't find it again," said another.

"No," said a third. "Rover never buried a bone. He's like us. He's too lazy to work so hard."

"Probably somebody tied him up with a tight rope so that he can't get away," said another.

"No," said the next. "Rover never moves fast enough to make anybody mad, and nobody except us could *want* that dog."

The family continued to lie in their yard. The sun shone around them, and the redbirds sang in the trees, but the day was less beautiful than before. The dog continued to bark unhappily, and this made them uncomfortable.

"Someone should go see whether or not Rover wants something," said the father. "A dog doesn't bark so much unless he needs help." He told his wife, "Sarah, you go find Rover."

"What did you say?" asked Sarah. "When we were married you told me that I could stop working, but I've worked every day of my married life. I run here and there for you. You live like a king. Now I'm too tired to move." Sarah put her head down in the grass again and closed her eyes.

"Don't be mad," said the father. "Sam," he said to his oldest son, "go find Rover."

"Pa, you know I'm engaged. While I'm lying here I'm thinking about all the troubles I'll have when I'm married. I'm too tired to move."

"All right, Sam," said the father. "Missy, you go take care of Rover."

"Pa, you said yourself that I weigh too little," said the oldest daughter. "I've been going in and out of the house all day to get things to eat. Now I'm too tired to move."

"I'm sorry, Missy," said the father. "Sally, princess, go find Rover."

His second daughter didn't open her eyes. "My shoes don't fit and my feet hurt," she said. "Besides, I'm too tired to move."

"Then don't worry, Sally," said the father. "Jim, find Rover for us, son. You can't have any dessert tonight unless you do."

"Ma didn't make any dessert for tonight," said the second son. "You can't trick me into leaving this comfortable spot of grass like that. I had to fight to get it and now I'm too tired to move. You couldn't pull me away with pliers. Somebody else around here should go."

"All right, Jim, all right. Freddy, can you find Rover?"

"Do you think I'll have to go very far to find him, Pa?" asked Freddy, the youngest child, looking at his toes.

"Not so far, son."

Slowly, Freddy got up. "I didn't plan on taking a long trip today," he said. "I'm too tired to move, too, but I'm sorry for Rover." He went across the yard and disappeared down the road.

After a while the dog stopped barking. The six people on the ground turned their heads to look at the road.

"Where are they?" asked Missy.

"Just a minute! I see them coming," said Jim.

Then, slowly, Freddy and Rover came into sight.

"What happened? Where was Rover?"

Freddy lay down, and Rover lay down beside him. Then Freddy said, "This dog was sitting in the middle of a briar patch, and he was too tired to move."

Vocabulary

air	log	redbird	to tie
to bury	mad	same	tight
crow	middle	to shine	trick
engaged	none	sight	unless
to fit	pliers	somewhat	to weigh
king	princess	sunshine	whether

Idioms

to take a trip   Just a minute!
around here   to tie up
to be mad   to come into sight
to make mad

Related Words

engaged (adj.)   to weigh (verb)   to trick (verb)
engagement (noun)   weight (noun)   trick (noun)

Opposites

king—queen
princess—prince
tight—loose
same—different

Structure

I. <u>LIKE</u>, <u>ALIKE</u>; <u>DIFFERENT</u> (<u>FROM</u>), <u>THE SAME</u> (<u>AS</u>)

A. *Read these sentences:*

My book is **like** your book.
   Our books are **alike**. [They may be a little bit different.]
A crow is **different from** a redbird.
   Crows and redbirds are **different**.
This piece of paper is **the same as** that piece.
   These pieces of paper are **the same**. [They are not at all different.]

B. *Choose the one of the above words or phrases that best fits the meaning of each of the following sentences.*

Example: This piece of chalk is _____ *that piece of chalk.*
   *This piece of chalk is **like** (or **the same as**) that piece of chalk.*

1. A king is _____ a queen.
2. The two redbirds are _____ .
3. This school is _____ other schools in the city.
4. A fat man and a thin man don't weigh _____ .
5. My pen is long, yours is short. Mine is _____ yours.
6. The sun is _____ the earth.
7. The blackboard in this room and the blackboard in the next room are _____ .
8. Dogs and cats are _____ , but one dog is _____ another dog.
9. I bought a thick blue notebook, and he did too. His notebook is _____ mine.
10. My sister likes to read all the time, but I prefer to go to the movies with friends. My sister and I are _____ .
11. The water in my glass tastes _____ the water in your glass.
12. This glass of water doesn't taste _____ the other.

13. From here all the stars look _____.
14. Children sometimes look _____ their parents.
15. The animals in my country are _____ the animals in the United States.

II. THE CONJUNCTIONS <u>WHETHER</u> AND <u>UNLESS</u>

A. The use of <u>whether</u> shows that there is a choice between two actions (often negative and affirmative) or two things. It is usually followed by <u>or</u>:

He wanted to see the house **whether** we did **or** not.
I don't know **whether** you want to go **or** stay.
He doesn't know **whether** it was an airplane **or** a bird.

B. <u>Unless</u> means <u>if</u> . . . <u>not</u>:

He will get the birds **unless** they fly away.
(He will get the birds **if** they do **not** fly away.)

You may write with a pencil **unless** you prefer a pen.
(You may write with a pencil **if** you do **not** prefer [to write with] a pen.)

C. Use either <u>whether</u> or <u>unless</u> to complete each of the following sentences:

1. You don't need a sweater _____ you feel cold.
2. I don't know _____ he wants the pencil or the book.
3. _____ it's too late, we shall hear the music on the radio.
4. We want to go for a walk _____ it rains or not.
5. Do you know _____ he is a singer or an actor?
6. I don't want to go _____ you do, too.
7. _____ he knows it or not, he must not speak in the library.
8. He didn't say _____ he prefers chicken or rabbit for dinner.
9. We'll have soup _____ you don't like it.
10. She will sing _____ we ask her to or not.

Conversation

Answer the following questions, using complete sentences:

1. How many people were in this lazy family?
2. How was the father different from the others?
3. Why didn't they chase the crows out of their cornfield?
4. What time of year was it?
5. What made them uncomfortable?
6. Who was engaged?
7. Were Sally's shoes the same size as her feet?
8. Why was Jim tired?
9. Who was the youngest?
10. Where did Freddy find Rover?
11. Will you go home this afternoon whether it rains or not?
12. Do you know anyone who is engaged?
13. What can you do with a pair of pliers?
14. Does a bird weigh very much?
15. Are crows heavier than rabbits?
16. Are there many crows around here?
17. Are we sitting on logs now?
18. Does anyone here have a pair of pliers?
19. Is there a pocket in your shirt?
20. Have you ever seen a princess?

Write or Tell

Tomorrow at Nine

An Interesting Trip

Dictation

Listen to, repeat, and then write each of the following sentences:

A dog named Rover made a lazy family uncomfortable be-cause he barked all afternoon. They knew that they couldn't rest unless one of them went to help Rover. The father, who was the laziest of all, wanted someone else to see whether Rover needed help or not. Rover was as lazy as the lazy family to whom he be-longed. He was too lazy to get up out of a briar patch.

Pronunciation

/ u /	/ U /	/ ks /
too	look	fox
coon	good	tricks
fool	full	six
flew	took	backs
truth	woods	example

/ u /	The coon, too, told the truth.
/ U /	Look at the good woods full of trees.
/ u, U /	The good coon took a walk in the woods, too.
/ ks /	For example, the fox knows six tricks.

Unit 10

Good Shooting

There was once a man who had a wife and a lot of children, but the day came when he no longer had any food for them to eat. That morning he said to his wife, "I have only one bullet left in my gun. I'm going to the woods and shoot something for us to eat. Make a fire in the stove, and put a pan of water on the stove to heat."

"That's a good idea," his wife told him. "Do go and shoot something. Shoot a duck or a possum."

The man went into the woods with his gun. Because he had only one bullet, he knew he must be very careful not to waste it on a small animal. He walked far into the woods, but he found nothing either large or small to shoot, and he began to worry.

Suddenly he saw a fat possum sitting on the branch of a tree. He was getting ready to shoot it when he saw a pond under the branch of the tree. On the pond was a flock of wild ducks. Beyond the pond was a big bear. There was a noise behind the man. He looked in back of him and saw some rabbits sitting on the ground.

He wanted to shoot all of these animals, but at first he didn't know how it could be done. Then he decided what to do, and he took careful aim with his gun.

He shot his one bullet. The bullet hit the branch that the possum was on, and the branch broke. As it fell into the pond, it killed the wild ducks, and the possum drowned in the pond. The bullet continued across the pond and killed the bear. The gun knocked the man down, and he fell on top of the rabbits. The rabbits were killed by his weight.

When the man stood up again, he went and got the bear. He carried the bear to the tree. Then he got the ducks and possum out of the water and put them with the bear. On top of them all, he put the rabbits. Then he saw he couldn't carry everything himself, so he went home for his horse and wagon.

When he got home, his wife said, "Where is the duck? Didn't you shoot anything? Did you lose your gun?"

He told his wife, "Don't ask me so many questions. Just keep the pan on the stove and the fire going. Soon there will be enough to eat."

Then he returned to the woods with his horse and wagon, and put the animals in the wagon. As he walked along the path home it began to rain. He said to his horse, "Come on. Come on, old boy. Hurry up."

When he got to the house, his wife said, "The water is hot, but where is the meat? Where did you go?"

Looking back toward the woods, the man saw the horse, but he didn't see his wagon. On the ground behind the horse lay the leather straps that connected it to the wagon. As far as the man could see, he saw only those leather straps. Then he knew what had happened: the straps had stretched in the rain, and the wagon was still in the woods.

"I think our dinner will get here this afternoon," he told his wife. "Don't worry."

He tied the horse to a tree near the door of the house, and went inside. Then he sat down to rest.

It didn't rain that afternoon, and the sun was hot. The leather straps behind the horse began to dry. As they dried, they shrank, and the wagon came out of the woods. It came nearer and nearer the house. About two o'clock the wagon was at the door, full of meat, and the family had a big dinner that evening.

Vocabulary

beyond	duck	to perform	quality
bullet	flock	performer	to receive
to drown	leather	pond	strap
to dry			wet

Idioms

in back of
to knock down
to go (home) for

Related Words

to perform (verb)
performer (noun)

to receive (verb)
receiver (noun)

Opposites

dry—wet
back—front
in back of—in front of
to receive—to give

Structure

I. THE PASSIVE VOICE

A. *Until now, you have mostly studied sentences in which the verb is in the active voice and the subject performs the action:*

The **man shot** the possum.

In the passive voice, the subject is acted upon or receives the action. The passive voice is formed by using the verb <u>to be</u> with the <u>past participle</u> of another verb. The performer of the action becomes the object of the preposition <u>by</u>.

The **possum was shot** by the man.

ACTIVE VOICE

Simple Present Tense:	The horse pulls the wagon.
	Does the horse pull the wagon?
Simple Past Tense:	The horse pulled the wagon.
	Did the horse pull the wagon?
Simple Future Tense:	The horse will pull the wagon.
	Will the horse pull the wagon?
Present Perfect Tense:	The horse has pulled the wagon.
	Has the horse pulled the wagon?

Structure (continued)

PASSIVE VOICE

Simple Present Tense:	The wagon is pulled by the horse. Is the wagon pulled by the horse?
Simple Past Tense:	The wagon was pulled by the horse. Was the wagon pulled by the horse?
Simple Future Tense:	The wagon will be pulled by the horse. Will the wagon be pulled by the horse?
Present Perfect Tense:	The wagon has been pulled by the horse. Has the wagon been pulled by the horse?

B. In each of the following sentences, put the verb into the passive voice, and change the order of the words as necessary:

Example: The man's wife cooked a rabbit.
A rabbit was cooked by the man's wife.

1. The boy throws the stone.
2. The old man will smoke his pipe.
3. We have finished all the exercises.
4. Three men have climbed the tallest mountain.
5. The thief stole a sheep from the field.
6. No one believes the story.
7. The father will punish the son for disobeying.
8. Finally the driver started the bus.
9. We have waked the old man who was dreaming.
10. The teacher changed the old chalk for new chalk.
11. They didn't break the window.
12. He has tied up the thief.
13. Has Melvin returned the horse?
14. Did he leave his dog behind?
15. Will the boy hurt the snake?
16. The girl teases her sister.
17. Have you whispered the word?
18. He dug the potatoes in his garden.

19. Is he growing corn?
20. He hunts animals in the woods.

II. PRACTICE WITH ARTICLES USED WITH COUNT AND MASS NOUNS

A. *An article always precedes a singular count noun. If the noun does not name a special thing, the indefinite article <u>a</u> or <u>an</u> is used with it:*

Please get **a pencil.**
Do you want **an apple?**

No article is used before a plural count noun that does not name a specific thing. The word **some** *is often used instead.*

Do you want **some apples?**
Pencils are not expensive.

If a count noun names a specific thing, the definite article **the** *is used:*

Take **the book** from your desk and read **the first page.**

The plural of a count noun naming a specific item also takes the article **the***:*

Where did you put **the keys?**

A mass noun that names a specific thing (or quality) takes the article **the***:*

The coffee in my cup is cold.

With a mass noun that does **not** *name a specific thing or quality no article is used:*

Water is the best drink.
Do you like to study **English?**

B. *Fill in the blank in each of the following sentences with a definite or indefinite article, if* necessary:

1. _____ ice is always colder than water.
2. She asked for _____ chalk that is on the desk.
3. _____ apples are usually red.

Structure (continued)

4. Please give me _____ sugar that is on the table.
5. Can you read _____ English that is in this book?
6. He would like to have _____ orange.
7. Is your friend _____ student?
8. Yes, he is _____ student whom you met yesterday.
9. I don't usually like to drink _____ tea.
10. _____ life is always interesting.
11. Do you know anything about _____ life of _____ people in Alaska?
12. He speaks both _____ Turkish and _____ English.
13. Is there _____ animal in the garden?
14. Did _____ raven speak to _____ hunter in the story?
15. _____ redbirds flew into the bag when he asked them to.

Conversation

Answer the following questions, using complete sentences:

1. How many children did the man in the story have?
2. What did he tell his wife to do?
3. How many bullets did he have?
4. Where was the possum sitting?
5. What killed the bear?
6. What did the man go home for?
7. How was the horse connected to the wagon?
8. What happened when it rained?
9. How did the wagon return to the house?
10. Did it rain in the afternoon?
11. If your clothes get wet in the rain, what must you do?
12. Where might a person drown?
13. Do you prefer dry or wet weather?
14. What does one need to shoot a bullet?

15. Have you ever seen a flock of ducks?
16. Do you have straps on your shoes?
17. What can live in a pond?
18. From what are shoes usually made?
19. Can you see beyond the classroom just now?
20. If you forget your book, do you go home for it?

Write or Tell

What Lies Beyond My Home

Some Uses of Leather

Dictation

Listen to, repeat, and then write each of the following sentences:

The man took a gun and went into the woods in back of his house. With one bullet he killed a possum, a flock of ducks, a bear, and some rabbits. Only the bear was shot by the man. Most of the others drowned. They were all put into a wagon, and then they were pulled to the man's house by the horse.

Pronunciation

/ ɝ /	/ ə /	/ ð /
her	but	there
worry	duck	leather
leather	gun	then
nearer	suddenly	this
girl	of	weather

/ ɝ /	Hurry nearer to the girl; don't worry.
/ ə /	But the duck suddenly saw the gun.
/ ð /	There is no good leather in this weather.
/ ɝ, ə /	The duck didn't worry the girl with the gun.

Unit 11

How the Coon Got His Supper

Once there was only a little food in the world and all the animals and fowls began to starve. Not even the buzzard could find enough to eat. Worst of all, no animal was safe from another.

Some of the biggest and strongest animals met to talk about their problems. They asked the elephant to be the chairman of the meeting because, as you know, an elephant does not care about eating other animals.

"Does anyone have an idea?" asked the elephant.

"I think the strongest animals should eat all the weakest ones," said the wildcat.

"Do *you* think that *you* are one of the strongest animals?" asked the tiger in an unfriendly voice.

"This kind of talk doesn't help us," said the elephant. "You should all give up meat and learn to eat vegetables like I do."

"Potatoes are all right for you," said the wolf, "but I like to eat rabbits. These days I can find only rats and mice in the field to take home to my cave."

Soon the meeting ended because no animal wanted to agree with another. The coon, who was listening in a corner, went to find his friend, the fox.

"The wolf has been catching mice," said the coon. "Let's go to the field where the mice are. If we help each other we can have supper tonight."

So they went to look for mice, but the field was very large, and the two friends didn't find anything there.

"We should dig," said the fox.

"That's too much work," the coon told him, "and you would find only worms. But I have a good idea. You should go and lie in the sun like a dead fox."

The fox was upset by this idea. "But I'm alive," he said. Still, he was very hungry, so he lay down and pretended to be dead. It was uncomfortable in the sun and the flies began to sit on him because he was so quiet.

The coon went to the edge of the field and sat on a stone. He called, "The fox is dead, the fox is dead."

Soon a whole family of mice, with uncles and cousins, came out of their holes. "Ee-ee, we don't believe it," said the big mice. "We don't, either," said the little mice. "He frightens us."

"You should bury that old fox. Bury him so deep that he can't get out and chase you," yelled the coon.

So all the big mice and little mice began to dig. They dug a hole with the fox in the middle of it. After a while they became tired. "Ee-ee. This is deep enough," they called.

"Can you climb out?" asked the coon.

"Yes, we can," yelled the mice.

"Then dig it deeper," yelled the coon.

So the mice dug deeper. They became tired again. "It's deep enough," they called.

"Can you climb out?"

"Ee-ee, no, we can't," said the little mice. "Ee-ee, yes, we can," called the big mice.

"Dig it deeper."

Then the mice dug a deeper hole. The fox lay inside it like he was dead. "That's enough. We've dug enough," called the mice.

"Can you climb out?" called the coon.

"Ee-ee, no, we can't," yelled the little mice. "Ee-ee, no, we can't," yelled the big mice.

"Then get up, friend fox, and get your supper!" yelled the coon, who jumped up from the stone and ran to the hole where his friend lay.

So the coon and the fox had meat for supper that night.

Vocabulary

buzzard	idea	rat	upset
cave	kind (of)	safe	wildcat
chairman	meeting	to starve	wolf
elephant	mouse	to suggest	world
fowl	potato	suggestion	worm
to frighten	problem	tiger	worst

Idioms

each other   to give up
(this) kind of talk   to agree with
worst of all (best of all, etc.)   to have an idea

Related Words

meeting (noun)
to meet (verb)

safe (adj.)
safely (adv.)
safety (noun)

Opposites

safe—unsafe
worst—best

Structure

I. <u>WHERE</u> AS A RELATIVE ADVERB

A. *Read these examples:*

What is a barn?
   A barn is a place **where** farmers put their cows.
What is a home?
   A home is a place **where** a family lives.
What is a school?
   A school is a building **where** students learn.

B. *Complete each of the following sentences by adding a clause introduced by <u>where</u>.*

Example: A kitchen is a room _____.
            A kitchen is a room where we can cook our food.

1. A woods is a place _____.
2. A porch is a part of a house _____.
3. A cemetery is a place _____.
4. A brier patch is a place _____.
5. A lake is a body of water _____.
6. A living room is a room _____.
7. A hospital is a building _____.

Structure (continued)

8. A garden is a place _____.
9. The field is a place _____.
10. A library is a building or a room _____.
11. A cave is a hole in a hill _____.
12. A city is a place _____.
13. The world is a place _____.
14. He went into the house _____.
15. This is the place _____.

II. TO AND FOR

A. *To and less often in order to may be used with the simple form of the verb to answer the question why.*

Why did you go? (Or, What did you go to do?)

I went **to buy** oranges.

I went **in order to get** my hat.

I went **to swim.**

B. *To show purpose, for is followed by a noun or gerund.*

Why did you go? (Or, What did you go for?)

I went / for oranges.

I went / for my hat.

I went / for swimming.

C. *Use to or for in each of the following sentences:*

1. I need a piece of chalk _____ write on the blackboard.
2. Are you going home _____ lunch?
3. He looked into his desk _____ find a pencil.
4. He looked into his desk _____ a pencil.
5. They met _____ talk about being better.
6. We come to class _____ learn English.
7. They come _____ English, too.
8. We are studying _____ take a test.
9. He works _____ money to go to the University.
10. He works _____ make money to go to the University.

Conversation

Answer the following questions, using complete sentences:

1. Who went to the meeting?
2. Why did the animals meet?
3. Who was the chairman of the meeting?
4. Why was he chairman?
5. What was the wildcat's idea?
6. What did the elephant suggest?
7. How did the coon learn about the place where the mice lived?
8. What did the fox have to do?
9. Why did the mice stop digging the first time?
10. Why did the coon tell them to dig deeper?
11. What do birds eat?
12. Do you believe that rabbits eat mice?
13. Are there elephants in your country?
14. Is a worm bigger than a snake?
15. Are we usually safe from tigers?
16. Are people usually frightened of mice?
17. What happens when people have nothing to eat?
18. Did you ever see the inside of a cave?
19. What kind of pencil do you have?
20. What is something you think is a problem?

Write or Tell

My Suggestions for a Better World

What I Think of Mice

Dictation

Listen to, repeat, and then write each of the following sentences:

The coon and the fox went to a field where the wolf usually caught mice. They went to catch some mice for their own supper. The problem was that none of the mice wanted to come out of the hole where he was safe. Then the fox pretended to be dead, and all the mice, with their cousins and uncles, came out to bury him.

Pronunciation

/ aU /	/ θ /
mouse	think
now	mouth
how	teeth
our	thirsty
house	three
	through

/ aU /   The mouse is now in our house.

/ θ /   The thirsty mouse had three teeth in its mouth.

Unit 12

Paul Bunyan

Who was Paul Bunyan?

Paul was born in Maine, but he didn't stay there. Maine is a small state, and Paul was a big baby. When he was three weeks old, he was too large for Maine. He kicked his feet, and ten miles of houses fell down.

"I am sorry, but you must take your child to another place," said the governor of Maine to Paul's father. So the Bunyan family decided to live in the West. In the West there were not so many houses.

When he was two years old, Paul started to take care of himself. He began to do amazing things. He pulled one end of a crooked road and made it straight. He drank a whole lake dry. A list of the amazing things he did before his eighteenth birthday is three hundred and fifty-two pages long—in small print.

When he was a man, Paul became a logger. He lived in a logging camp, and was the greatest logger in the country. But sometimes he was lonely. In the evenings, he sat in front of his house, combing his beard with a small tree, while the other loggers played cards.

Then one evening he heard a noise.

"That's a woman yelling," he said to himself. "She's louder than a wildcat."

He stepped to the top of the mountain behind his house and looked down. There was a woman sitting in a tall redwood tree. That redwood tree was about a mile high.

"What's your name?" called Paul.

"Carrie," she yelled back.

"What's the trouble?"

"There's a bear."

"Where is it?"

"It's under the tree. I'm afraid of bears," she yelled.

Paul laughed. The woman was much bigger than the bear. Women are strange, he thought. He went down the mountain to the bottom of the tree, picked up the bear, and carried it to the other side of the forest. Then he returned to Carrie, who still sat in the top of the tree.

"You had better come down now," Paul said.

"All right, if the bear is gone," yelled Carrie, and she jumped. When she hit the ground, she made a hole a mile deep and half a mile wide. People on the other side of the world felt the ground shake under them.

Paul's big heart began to knock against his chest. That Carrie is a fine woman, he thought. "How are you?" he asked, calling down into the hole. He was afraid that she was hurt.

Carrie just laughed and climbed out. When she stood beside Paul, she was almost as tall as he was.

"I like you," Paul said. "You can yell. You can jump—and you don't look bad. You're big, too. Honey, will you marry me? Will you be my little wife?"

Carrie had never heard such sweet words before, and she enjoyed them. "Yes, I'll marry you," she said.

They say

> Needles and pins,
> Needles and pins,
> When a man marries
> His trouble begins.

Paul was big, but he was no exception.

Vocabulary

card	forest	logger	pin
chest	governor	loud	print
crooked	hole	Maine	redwood
deep	honey	to omit	speech
exception			such

Idioms

a mile high

a mile deep

half a mile wide

the other side of (something)

They say . . .

Related Words

logger (noun)	pin (noun)	speech (noun)
log (noun)	to pin (verb)	to speak (verb)
loud (adj.)	print (noun)	
loudly (adv.)	to print (verb)	
loudness (noun)		

Opposites

crooked—straight
loud—soft, quiet

Structure

I. THE AUXILIARY HAD BETTER

A. *Had better may be used with the simple form of a verb for present or future time. (The contracted form is more commonly used in spoken English.) Had better means almost the same as should.*

We had better go now, or we shall be late for class.
(We'd)
She had better comb her hair before her friend comes.
(She'd)
Had we better take our coats?

To form a sentence in the negative had better is used with not and the simple form of the verb:

He had better not walk in the rain.
(He'd)
You had better not forget your book.
(You'd)
Hadn't we better close the window?

B. *Complete each of the following sentences, first using had better and then had better not. Use contractions in oral practice:*

Example: You _____ go home now.
        You had (You'd) better go home now.
        You had (You'd) better not go home now.

1. I think that she _____ jump.
2. _____ we _____ study English tonight?

3. _____ they _____ stop playing cards now?
4. You _____ keep on working until you finish.
5. She _____ worry about her son.
6. We _____ believe what he says.
7. She _____ write the answer to the question.
8. You _____ pick up that piece of paper.
9. They _____ hide under the table.
10. _____ I _____ turn on the light?

C. *Answer each of the following questions, using* <u>had better</u> *in your answer:*

Example: *Had I better write with a pen?*
Yes, you had better write with a pen.

1. Had I better tell him the answer?
2. Had we better begin this exercise again?
3. Had they better go home now?
4. Hadn't your friend better stop working?
5. Hadn't you better ask her to come with us?
6. Hadn't he better get up now?
7. Had she better complain so much?
8. Hadn't we better knock on a door that is closed?
9. Had I better climb the tree to get the cat?
10. Had I better put on my hat now?

II. THE PASSIVE VOICE: THE PERFORMER OF THE ACTION OMITTED

A. *When the performer of the action is not important for the meaning of a sentence, it may be omitted from sentences with verbs in the passive voice:*

This mountain **is** very often **climbed**.
[Who climbs it is not so interesting or important.]
It **is believed** that the moon is round.

B. *In each of the following sentences put the verb into the passive voice:*

Structure (continued)

> *Example: Carrie* _____ (*hurt*) _____ *when she jumped.* (*past tense*)
> *Carrie **was hurt** when she jumped.*

1. The bear _____ (carry) _____ to the other side of the woods. (past)
2. Something _____ (drop) _____ from the airplane. (past)
3. The thief _____ (catch) _____ before he left the city. (past)
4. Their son _____ (send) _____ to college for seven years. (past)
5. Books _____ (borrow) _____ from the library every day. (present)
6. The newspaper _____ (bring) _____ to our door every morning. (present)
7. The candy _____ (divide) _____ among the children. (past)
8. The wagon _____ (pull) _____ from the woods to the house. (past)
9. This soup _____ (make) _____ two hours ago. (past)
10. This story _____ (call) _____ *Paul Bunyan.* (present)

Conversation

Answer the following questions, using complete sentences:

1. Where was Paul Bunyan born?
2. Why did his family have to leave that state?
3. How long is the list of the amazing things he did?
4. When did he become a logger?
5. What did he use to comb his beard?
6. What kind of tree was Carrie sitting in?
7. What was under the tree?

8. How did she come down from the tree?
9. Where did people feel the ground shake?
10. Why did Paul like Carrie?
11. What do people usually use to comb their hair?
12. Is the print on this page small or large?
13. Is the road in front of the school straight or crooked?
14. What is on the other side of the road from the school?
15. How wide is the road?
16. Do you sometimes pin your papers together?
17. Have you seen the list of words in the back of this book?
18. How many uses for pins can you think of?
19. Do you think Carrie was an amazing woman?
20. Do you know of another amazing man like Paul?

Write or Tell

The Other Side of the Street

The Road from Here to . . . (name of a Town or City)

Dictation

Listen to, repeat, and then write each of the following sentences:

Paul heard a loud noise from the other side of the mountain. He thought that he had better go to help. A woman was frightened and sat in the top of a tall redwood tree. "You'd better come down," said Paul. But there was a bear under the tree and she didn't want to come down until the bear was taken away. When she finally jumped, she made a hole a mile deep. Paul was amazed that she was such a strong woman.

Pronunciation

/ ɔɪ /	/ θ /	/ ð /
b<u>oy</u>	<u>th</u>ing	<u>th</u>en
n<u>oi</u>se	<u>th</u>ree	<u>th</u>is
v<u>oi</u>ce	eigh<u>th</u>teen	fa<u>th</u>er
p<u>oi</u>nt	<u>th</u>ought	<u>th</u>an
sp<u>oi</u>l	ear<u>th</u>	o<u>th</u>er
		<u>th</u>ere

/ ɔɪ /   "I hear a v<u>oi</u>ce," said the n<u>oi</u>sy b<u>oy</u>.

/ θ /   <u>Th</u>ree <u>th</u>ings on ear<u>th</u> I like, he <u>th</u>ought.

/ ð /   <u>Th</u>is fa<u>th</u>er is taller <u>th</u>an <u>th</u>e o<u>th</u>er.

/ θ, ð /   <u>Th</u>is is <u>th</u>e <u>th</u>irteen<u>th</u> time <u>th</u>at fa<u>th</u>er saw <u>th</u>e <u>th</u>ing.

Unit 13

The Unlucky Wedding Day

People say that somewhere in the northern Appalachian Mountains, there is a place where people never grow old. Perhaps this is true. There are many stories about men who were lost there for twenty or thirty years. When these men returned to their homes, they were no older than they had been thirty years before.

Once there lived in a mountain village a young man named Hans. He was a strong, handsome young man, and he had a warm heart. He fell in love with a girl named Margaret, who lived in another village across the mountains.

When Hans and Margaret became engaged, the day they planned for their wedding was in the spring. On that day the mountains were full of flowers, and the trees had new green leaves.

On the morning of his wedding day, Hans put on a new coat, a soft black hat, and shoes of fine leather. Then he began to walk across the mountains to his Margaret. He thought about the afternoon when he was going to be with her forever, and he sang to himself as he walked.

When he had gone about half of the way to Margaret's village, a storm came through the mountains. The sky became black, and rain followed thunder and lightning. Owls cried from the trees, and Hans could hear the howling of wolves in the darkness. But he was not afraid. He thought only of Margaret, who was waiting for him.

But the sky became so black that soon Hans was lost among the trees. He went this way and that, but he couldn't find the right path.

Suddenly beside him there was a small man with a big red nose and a tall hat. "Come with me," the man said. "I shall take you to safety."

Hans followed him through the forest, and they came out into a green valley where there was no storm. In the middle of the meadow was a chair of gold, and on the chair sat a king. He was young, and there were only young and beautiful people around him. They walked, arm in arm, across the grass with quiet smiles on their faces, as though they were asleep. Hans went to the king.

"Where am I?" he asked.

"You are in the land where men never become old," said the king. "Stay with us."

"I can't stay," said Hans. "This is my wedding day, and I must go to my bride."

"But you must stay with us until the storm is over," said the king. "When the weather is better, you will be shown the path."

Hans remained in the meadow for a time, walking among the quiet, peaceful people. A man on each side took his arm, but no one spoke to him. Then he pulled his arms away and went again to the king.

"I must go to my bride," he cried. "Please help me."

"You won't be happy," the king said. "You had better not go. Stay with us. Here we are forever young and happy."

"I don't want to be young forever," said Hans. "I must go. Margaret is waiting for me."

"Go then," said the king, "but you will want to come back to us again."

The man with the big red nose led Hans from the meadow into the forest, where he showed him the path to Margaret's village. The storm had stopped, and the sun was shining. Hans told the little man good-bye and went quickly along his way. The birds sang; the grass was green; the sun was warm; and Hans's heart was full of love. He hoped that Margaret was not frightened because he was so late.

Finally he came to the village. Was it the same as it had been a few days before? Weren't there more houses? Now the street was made of cobblestones, not of earth. In the yard in front of Margaret's house sat a little old woman.

Hans stared at her. He didn't know her—or did he? He stood before the house until the old woman saw him. Slowly she stood up and came to him. Her face was pale.

"Hans," she said.

"My name is Hans. Where is Margaret? Where is my bride?"

"Do you really want your Margaret now?" she asked.

"Of course," he said, and looked toward the house. "Is she inside?"

"I am Margaret," said the old woman.

His face grew as pale as hers. "No, no. I mean my—"

"I am your Margaret," she said. "I have waited for you for sixty years."

"But there was a storm in the mountains . . . I stayed only an hour in a dry meadow . . . There was a little man . . ." he began.

"No, not one hour—sixty years, Hans."

Hans knew that she spoke the truth. He took her feeble old hand in his strong young one. "What shall we do?" he asked sadly. "My life is nothing without you."

"I am too old for you in this life, Hans. Perhaps we shall meet in the next world."

Suddenly Hans laughed. "I know what we must do, Margaret," he said. "We must find the place from which I have come. There we shall be young together. There everyone is young, and the minutes are years."

The old woman left her village and followed Hans deep into the Appalachian Mountains. They never returned. Some say they found the place where men never grow old; some say they died in the mountains. Perhaps one day we shall learn the truth.

Vocabulary

among	frightened	over (ended)	to stare (at)
arm	land	owl	storm
bride	to lead	pale	thunder
cobblestones	lost	peaceful	valley
forever	meadow	pile	wedding

Idioms

to grow old	to be lost
(to go) this way and that way	arm in arm
to be over (ended)	wedding day
to be found	to fall in love with
to grow pale	the next world

Related Words

lost (adj.)	thunder (noun)
to lose (verb)	to thunder (verb)

Opposites

lost—found
pale—dark

Structure

I. MORE PRACTICE WITH INFINITIVES

A. *After some verbs, the direct object may be an infinitive phrase:*

He tried **to hit** the ball.
I expected **to see** the teacher.
She got up **to open** the door.

Many infinitives take an object themselves, but some do not:

The man wanted **to sing**.
Mary wants **to sleep**.

B. *Form sentences by connecting each of the clauses at the left with the correct infinitive phrase at the right:*

1. Mary asked	to feed his family.
2. I began	to walk.
3. John decided	to be cowboys.
4. Old Lady Simpson forgot	to go with us.
5. Her daughters helped	to catch the ball.
6. The child learned	to salt the soup.
7. The people paid	to leave the garden.
8. The teacher planned	to count my money.
9. The angry man said	to sing a song.
10. The father worked	to give a test.
11. The student stood	to pick up the people.
12. The children pretended	to study his English lesson.
13. The bus stopped	to see the movie.
14. The player jumped	to read the exercises.
15. The actor started	to clean the house.

Structure (continued)

> **C.** *Some verbs may have both a noun or pronoun and an infinitive phrase as object:*
>
> Mary asked **us to play** with her.
> She doesn't like **John to smoke** cigarettes.
> I want **you to visit** us one day.
>
> **D.** *Make good sentences by connecting each of the clauses at the left with the correct noun or pronoun object and infinitive phrase:*
>
> *Example: He asked the girl to marry him.*

1. He asked	the students	to pick up the pencil.
2. She will expect	me	to wear to the dance.
3. The thief stole	his father	to come home early.
4. She sewed	our children	to salt the soup.
5. The teacher taught	his son	to marry him.
6. I told	us	to get the mule.
7. My mother wants	my father	to do the work.
8. My husband likes	her daughters	to make a cake for her.
9. His boss pays	the girl	to send him money.
10. John wrote	the cats	to eat.
11. The preacher expected	her mother	to go to class now.
12. The girl wanted	him	to speak English.
13. Mrs. Simpson expected	the sheep	to give me some money.
14. The farmer sent	you	to clean the house.
15. I called	the dress	to go away.

II. <u>TO MAKE</u> AND <u>TO DO</u>; <u>TO BEAT</u> AND <u>TO HIT</u>; <u>TO BRING</u> AND <u>TO TAKE</u>; <u>TO LEND</u> AND <u>TO BORROW</u>

A. *Practice the following verb forms:*

He **is making** a table.
She **is doing** her homework.
She **is beating** the rug.
The car **hit** a tree.
He **is bringing** his son to school.
He **is taking** the book to his home.
He **is lending** her his book.
He **is borrowing** a book from the library.

B. *Choose one of the verbs listed above to complete each of the following sentences:*

Example: When you come to school tomorrow, don't forget to **bring** *your pencil.*

1. "Please _____ me your mule to ride," said the boy.
2. My wife _____ all the housework at home every day.
3. We must _____ the sick boy to a hospital.
4. Did the postman _____ you a letter today?
5. The rain is _____ against the window.
6. He threw a stone at the chicken, but did not _____ it.
7. Do you know how to _____ soup?
8. He _____ the bear with a bullet.
9. My pen is here now, but I shall _____ it home with me.
10. Why don't you have your book? Did someone _____ it?
11. I don't have any money for the bus. Will you _____ me some?
12. He always _____ his best work in a quiet room.
13. Did you ever _____ your family to the country?
14. He _____ the dog until it ran away.
15. What do you usually _____ in the afternoon?

Conversation

Answer the following questions, using complete sentences:

1. Where did Hans live?
2. For what time of year did Hans and Margaret plan their wedding?
3. What did Hans wear on his wedding day?
4. Why did he become lost in the mountains?
5. Who was in the middle of the meadow?
6. Why did the king want Hans to stay?
7. How was the weather when Hans left the meadow?
8. In what ways was Margaret's village different?
9. How long had Hans been gone?
10. How had Margaret changed?
11. Have you ever heard an owl?
12. Is it possible to live forever?
13. Do you like the sound of thunder?
14. Do you enjoy a quiet, peaceful evening at home?
15. Do people usually wear fine clothes on their wedding day?
16. Do we often stare at strange things?
17. When will this lesson be over?
18. Do you prefer light blue or dark blue?
19. What grows in a meadow?
20. When do you think a person begins to grow old?

Write or Tell

A Wedding I've Seen

A Peaceful Place

Dictation

Listen to, repeat, and then write each of the following sentences:

Hans lived in a small village on the side of a mountain. He loved a girl named Margaret, and no one wanted to marry as much as he did. On his wedding day he became lost in the mountains far from Margaret's village. He stayed in a peaceful meadow for sixty years, but he didn't grow old. Perhaps he and Margaret are in the meadow now, or perhaps they are lost forever among the trees of the forest.

Pronunciation

/ hw /	/ ʃ /	/ tʃ /
somewhere	she	chair
when	shining	Appalachian
what	shall	child
why	shoes	question
which	finish	much

/ hw /   When we know which way, we'll go somewhere.

/ ʃ /   She shall finish making the shoes in the shining sun.

/ tʃ /   The child in the chair asks questions about the Appalachians.

/ ʃ, tʃ /   She'll put the child's shoes in the chair.

Unit 14

John Henry

John Henry was born during a thunderstorm. The thunder had a noise like hammers on steel. Soon after he was born, he spoke.

"I'm hungry," he said.

"Do you want some milk, son?" asked his father.

"Milk is for babies," said John Henry. "Don't you hear my man's voice? Don't you know I have a hungry soul? Bring me three pans of peas. Bring me ten chickens and three dishes of cabbage. Bring me a mountain of candy for my sweet tooth."

"Your eyes are bigger than your stomach," said his father. "You talk too much."

108

But John Henry's mother and father got all the food together. They put it on seven tables in the yard. John Henry's father looked at the food and shook his head. Then he called his son.

"It's all there in the yard, son," he said. "It's on seven tables."

John Henry walked to the tables and began to eat. The food disappeared.

"He ate all that food," said his father, amazed.

"Of course I did," said John Henry. "Now I'm going to sleep for nine hours."

He slept for nine hours—exactly nine hours. When he woke up, he said, "I'm hungry. My soul is hungry. Bring me thirteen possums and lots of sweet potatoes. Bring me ninety pieces of bread and three dishes of honey."

His parents didn't ask any questions. They got the food for their son.

For several months, John Henry slept and ate, slept and ate. Then one day he found a hammer and a piece of steel. He began to hit the steel with the hammer. It made a sound like big church bells or a thunderstorm in the hills.

The little boy stopped hitting the steel and smiled at his father. "I'm happy," he said. "My soul isn't hungry now."

"You are going to use a hammer when you are big," said his father.

"Yes," said John Henry. "I'm going to live and die with a hammer in my hand."

When John Henry grew up, he became a cotton picker. He had a wife named Polly Ann whom he loved more than words can tell. She had eyes like stars, and dancing feet. But John Henry still had a hungry soul. He sang sad songs, and his eyes looked far away.

"Your home isn't here, John Henry," his wife often said.

One day John Henry said, "You are right, Polly Ann. This isn't my home. I think we should go away. We should say good-bye to this place."

So John Henry and Polly Ann left their home. They looked in one place and another for a new and better one, but when the hunger came again to John Henry's soul, they moved on.

One day, from far away, John Henry heard the sound of hammers on steel. He took Polly Ann's hand, and they ran to where the men were working.

There John Henry saw a mountain of stone. The men were making a railroad tunnel through the mountain. First they hammered steel into the stone to make holes. Then they put dynamite into the holes and blasted away the stone.

John Henry went to the foreman and said, "I'm big and strong. Give me a hammer, and I'll hammer more steel than nine other men together."

"Here's a man with a big mouth," said the foreman. "Give him a hammer!"

John Henry began to hammer steel, and he sang as he hammered. The other men laughed, but he didn't hear them.

After a time the foreman said, "Stop, John Henry. I want to see what you have done." The other men went near to see, too. They saw that John Henry had hammered more steel than ten other men together. No one laughed now.

"Work for me," said the foreman, "and I'll give you what you want."

"I just want a bigger hammer," said John Henry.

So John Henry began to hammer steel, and his soul was not hungry any more. He was a happy man. Every day people heard his hammer from miles away. He and Polly Ann had found their home.

Then one day a salesman came to the foreman. He had a steam drill to sell. "This steam drill is faster than twenty men," he said. "You don't have to feed it, and it doesn't have to rest. You can do a lot more work with it than you can with a man."

"I don't know," said the foreman. "I have the best steel hammering man in the world. I like him. Let's have a race between your steam drill and my John Henry. If the steam drill wins, I'll buy it. If John Henry wins, you'll give us five hundred dollars."

"I know John Henry is good, but he's only a man," said the salesman. "Let's have a nine-hour race."

So the foreman went to John Henry. "Will you race a steam drill for nine hours, John Henry?" he asked. "You'll get a reward if you win."

"Of course I'll race it," said John Henry. "I'll race it, and I'll win. I'm a steel hammering man. I'm only happy with a hammer in my hand. I'm going to live and die with a hammer in my hand."

The day for the race came. People came from far and near to see it. On one side was the steam drill, and on the other side was John Henry. The foreman threw his hat into the air, and the race began. The steam drill began to cut the stone, and John Henry began to hammer. His hammer rang like silver and gold.

One hour passed, and two. John Henry was quicker than the drill. Sometimes he stopped and drank water which Polly Ann gave him, but he didn't slow down. Six hours, seven hours, eight hours—and he didn't slow down. But in the ninth hour, John Henry began to tire.

"How are you, John Henry?" people asked.

"The stone is hard," said John Henry, "but that steam drill won't win. I'll die with my hammer in my hand first."

The crowd was quiet in the last minutes of the race. The only sounds were the chug-chug of the steam drill and the ring of John Henry's hammer.

Then the foreman looked at his watch and said, "The race is over."

The drill stopped. People saw that John Henry had made three holes more than the steam drill. Everyone was happy except the salesman—and John Henry. John Henry lay on the ground, and his pretty Polly Ann was holding his head.

"Give me a drink of cold water before I die," he said.

Polly Ann gave him some water and kissed him good-bye. He lay very still: the only sound was Polly Ann's crying.

They buried John Henry near the mountain with his hammer in his hand.

Vocabulary

bell	foreman	to ring	thunderstorm
to blast	hammer	salesman	to tire
candy	pea	sense	tongue
cotton	picker	star	to touch
dynamite	railroad	steam drill	tunnel
finger		steel	

Idioms

sweet tooth
to grow up
to move on
one place and another (etc.)
to get (things, people) together

Related Words

to blast (verb)	hammer (noun)	railroad (noun)
blast (noun)	to hammer (verb)	rail (noun)
drill (noun)	picker (noun)	to tire (verb)
to drill (verb)	to pick (verb)	tired (adj.)
		tiredly (adv.)

Opposites

to move on—to stay

Structure

I. PRACTICE WITH VERBS OF THE SENSES

A. *With our eyes we see, look, and watch.*

He **is looking at** the picture.
He **sees** many things from the window.
Many people **are watching** the ball game.

With our noses we smell and breathe.

He **smells** the soup.
"**Breathe** deeply, please."

With our tongues or mouths we taste and eat.

He **is tasting** the soup.
They **are eating** dinner.

With our ears we hear and listen.

He **heard** a noise.
She **is listening** to the music.

With our fingers we touch and feel.

He **can touch** his toes.
She **is feeling** the cloth.

B. *Use the correct form of see, look, or watch in each of the following sentences:*

1. He _____ at the clock and _____ that it was six o'clock.
2. She wants to _____ us again tomorrow.
3. I _____ the cat while she caught the mouse.
4. We _____ into the water and _____ many fish.
5. He _____ television every night.
6. Can you _____ in the dark?
7. Please _____ at the blackboard.
8. The little girl is _____ her baby brother.

Structure (continued)

Use the correct form of <u>smell</u> or <u>breathe</u> in each of the following sentences:

1. People cannot _____ under water.
2. Can you _____ the roses that are under the window?
3. I know she is making supper, but I can't _____ it.
4. At seven o'clock he opens the window and _____ the morning air.
5. We could _____ the fire before we saw it.

Use the correct form of <u>taste</u> or eat in each of the following sentences:

1. He always _____ his soup before he _____ it.
2. Do you _____ the salt in the soup?
3. Yesterday I _____ two big red apples.
4. Have you ever _____ sweet potatoes?
5. Please _____ the candy. If you don't like it, you don't have to _____ it.

Use the correct form of <u>hear</u> or <u>listen</u> in each of the following sentences:

1. I can _____ the radio but I don't want to _____ to it.
2. One should _____ before he speaks.
3. When we are quiet, we can _____ the bells.
4. We need to _____ to the teacher's pronunciation.
5. For a long time he stood _____ to the birds.

Use the correct form of <u>touch</u> or <u>feel</u> in each of the following sentences:

1. She jumped when she _____ the hot stove.
2. He _____ under his bed for his shoes.
3. The doctor _____ her arm to see if the bone was broken.
4. His brother smokes, but John won't _____ cigarettes.
5. He _____ the box before he opened it.

II. NOUNS FORMED FROM VERBS

A. *Certain verbs may add -er to form nouns.*

He **teaches** our class. He is a **teacher**.
He often **climbs** mountains. He is a mountain **climber**.
He **plays** football. He is a football **player**.

B. *Form nouns from the verbs in the list below. Choose the best noun to complete each of the following sentences.*

Example: He is the best ball _____ in our town.
He is the best ball **catcher** *in our town.*

borrow	kill	follow
knock	catch	love
jump	complain	smoke
hunt	lend	

1. My brother likes cigarettes very much. He is a heavy
   _____.
2. He used to like sports. He was a good high _____.
3. Margaret did not see her _____ for sixty years.
4. He doesn't like to lead, but he is a good _____.
5. On the door was a silver _____.
6. He was a thief, but he was no _____.
7. John gave me his book to read. He is the _____, and
   I am the _____.
8. The _____ shot a bear by the pond.
9. "The meat is too cold, and the potatoes too hot," said
   the _____.

Conversation

Answer the following questions, using complete sentences:

1. What was the first thing John Henry said?
2. What food did his parents get together?
3. Did they believe that he could eat all the food?
4. When John Henry used a hammer, what was the noise like?
5. Who was Polly Ann?

Conversation (continued)

6. What were the men doing by the mountain?
7. How much steel could John Henry hammer?
8. Who told the foreman about the steam drill?
9. How many hours did John Henry race the steam drill?
10. How did he die?
11. Is anything in this room made of steel?—of cotton?
12. Did the bell ring just now?
13. Are there any railroad tunnels in this country? Where?
14. Is it easy to get things together in the morning?
15. Do you have a sweet tooth?
16. Did you grow up near here?
17. What does a foreman do?
18. When you tire while working, do you slow down?
19. What are peas like?
20. What kind of races have you seen?

Write or Tell

Sounds I Like to Hear

A Trip on the Railroad

Dictation

Listen to, repeat, and then write each of the following sentences:

John Henry loved hard work. When he grew up, he hammered steel. His hammer made a noise like a thunderstorm. When he found work on the railroad tunnel, he and his wife were happy. Then he raced a steam drill while a crowd of people watched. The drill did not tire, but John Henry did.

Pronunciation

/ aU /	/ l /	/ r /
mountain	little	hammer
sound	tunnel	war
mouth	steel	star
down	bell	bear
now	railroad	tire
	long	wrong

/ aU /   Let's go down the mountain now.
/ l /   We traveled along the steel rails.
/ r /   He tired with the wrong hammer.
/ l, r /   The little bear walked near the wrong bell.

Unit 15

Joe and Sam in the Country

Joe and Sam moved to the country from the city because they thought the more fresh air they had the better. They didn't know anything about plants and animals, but they began working for a farmer who had two thousand sheep. Joe and Sam had to take the sheep to the fields in the morning and bring them back to the farm in the evening.

The first evening they went to the farmer. They were tired out and covered with dust.

"We're sorry, but we can't work for you," they told him. "One day here is enough. It's better to die in the city."

"What's the matter?" asked the farmer. "You just have to walk beside the sheep all day, or sit and watch them eating grass. It's a quiet job."

"The *big* sheep don't run. They're tame," said Joe.

"But those *little* lambs made us run races all the time," said Sam. "We almost lost two or three of those wild babies, but they are all in your barn now."

The farmer knew he had only sheep, no lambs.

"How many sheep did you bring back from the fields?" he asked.

"Two thousand," said Joe.

"How many lambs?" asked the farmer.

"Sixty-eight. I hope that is all you had," said Sam.

So the farmer went down to the sheep barn to count his sheep. He saw that his two thousand sheep were there; but also, sitting close together in a corner, there were sixty-eight frightened rabbits!

      ❀   ❀   ❀

Joe and Sam listened to lots of stories about snakes, but they never saw one. People said that rattlesnakes were the most dangerous, but that no snakes were really good snakes. The more people talked about snakes, the more Joe and Sam thought about them. They always carried big sticks.

One day they decided to visit the farm of a friend. After they had walked a long way, they became lost. Then they passed a farmer plowing his field and asked him the way to their friend's house.

"Go down that way," he said, pointing. "Walk across the field. Go over the old rail fence, and then along the path through the woods."

"Thank you," said Joe, and he and Sam started across the field.

"Be careful, though," shouted the farmer. "I killed a big rattlesnake by the fence today. Maybe his mate is still there."

Joe and Sam almost died of fright. They held on to each other, and one looked left, and the other looked right as they walked slowly toward the rail fence. There they looked up and down, but they didn't see anything strange.

Sam was first, so he climbed over the fence. On the other side he turned around to examine it. He saw what was really Joe's big toe coming through a hole in a rail.

"Don't move!" yelled Sam. "I see a snake!"

Joe's eyes grew big, and he didn't move his little finger—or his big toe. Sam hit the toe with the big stick he always carried.

"Oh-h-h," cried Joe. "Hit it again, Sam. It bit me!"

Vocabulary

to bite	to examine	lamb	sound
close	fresh	mate	stick
correlative	fright	matter	though
country	healthy	maybe	toe
dust	to hope	plant	

Idioms

to work for (someone)
to be tired out
what's the matter?

to ask the way (to)
close together
to hold on (to)

Related Words

to bite (verb)
bite (noun)

dust (noun)
to dust (verb)
dusty (adj.)

to examine (verb)
examination (noun)

fright (noun)
to frighten (verb)
frightened (adj.)

healthy (adj.)
health (noun)

to hope (verb)
hope (noun)

plant (noun)
to plant (verb)

Opposites

country—city
close—far
healthy—sick

Structure

I. COMPLEMENTS FOLLOWING <u>BECOME</u>, <u>FEEL</u>, <u>LOOK</u>, <u>SEEM</u>, <u>SMELL</u>, <u>SOUND</u>, AND <u>TASTE</u>

A. *The verbs listed above are often followed by an adjective:*

He **became** tired.
Do you **feel** better?
John **looks** unhappy.

B. *These verbs may be followed by <u>like</u> and a noun or pronoun:*

This paper **smells** like roses.
I think Matthew is on the telephone, but it doesn't **sound** like him.
This candy **tastes** like honey.
She **is becoming** like her mother.

C. *Complete each of the following sentences, first by using an adjective, and second by using <u>like</u> followed by a noun or pronoun.*

Example: Joe looks _____.
  1) Joe looks afraid.
  2) Joe looks like his brother.

1. The song sounds _____.
2. This apple tastes _____.
3. The cloth feels _____.
4. You look _____.
5. Those flowers smell _____.

Structure (continued)

      6. Sam seems _____.
      7. She didn't know that the soup tasted _____.
      8. I didn't eat any, but it smelled _____.
      9. We listened to him sing because he sounded _____.
     10. He touched the stone, and it felt _____.

II. The ... the

A. *The correlative adverbs the . . . the may be followed by other modifying words to compare two things or actions:*

The bigger the apple (is) **the happier** the child (is).
The more we eat **the less** we want.
The longer he waits **the angrier** he becomes.
The sooner we finish **the better** (it will be).

B. *Connect each of the following sentences with the . . . the and the comparative forms of the adverbs or adjectives given:*

*Example: We see **much**. We want **much**.*
      The more we see the more we want.

      1. He walks **fast**. He becomes **tired**.
      2. She sings **much**. It sounds **bad**.
      3. It smells **good**. It tastes **good**.
      4. He drank **much** water. He wanted **much**.
      5. He went **far**. He became **lost**.
      6. We study **much**. We learn **much**.
      7. He travels **much**. He wants to go **far**.
      8. He smokes **much**. He feels **sick**.
      9. She comes home **late**. Her mother is **worried**.
    10. The street is **wide**. It is **safe**.
    11. The dew is **heavy**. The grass is **wet**.
    12. He yelled **much**. She became **angry**.
    13. She complained **much**. He listened **little**.
    14. He stayed **long**. The cats seemed **big**.
    15. He became **old**. He was **mean**.

Conversation

Answer the following questions, using complete sentences:

1. How many sheep did the farmer have?
2. What did Joe and Sam have to do with the sheep?
3. Why did they become tired?
4. What did the farmer find sitting close together?
5. Did Joe and Sam ever see a snake?
6. Why did they always carry a stick?
7. Who helped them when they were lost?
8. Where did the farmer kill a rattlesnake?
9. What did Sam think was a snake?
10. Why did Joe think that the snake bit him?
11. Are the desks in this room close together?
12. How many big toes does a person have on each foot?
13. What is a hen's mate called?
14. Do you enjoy seeing plants in a house?
15. Do you prefer to bite a sour or a sweet apple?
16. If a person is lost, what should he do?
17. When there is no rain for a long time are the streets dusty?
18. If you want fresh air in a room, what must you do?
19. My pen won't write. Do you know what's the matter with it?
20. Will you go to the country or the city for your vacation?

Write or Tell

Something Frightening

Why I Prefer the City (Country)

Dictation

Listen to, repeat, and then write each of the following sentences:

Joe didn't know anything about the country, and Sam was like Joe. He didn't know anything, either. They always carried sticks because they felt afraid of snakes. The closer they came to the fence the more afraid they were. Joe's toe looked like a snake, so Sam hit it with his stick. They think that the sooner they return to the city the better.

Pronunciation

/ kw /	/ ŋ /
quick	rang
quiet	bring
queen	anything
question	evening

/ kw /   The quiet queen quickly asked a question.
/ ŋ /   Don't bring anything this evening.

GLOSSARY OF
GRAMMATICAL TERMS

Adjective An adjective modifies (describes) a noun or pronoun. See **Complement, Degree, Participle.**

> Articles: *a, an, the*
> Possessive adjectives: *my, your, his,* etc.
> Relative adjective: *whose*

Adverb An adverb modifies a verb, an adjective, or another adverb. See **Clause.**

> Correlative adverbs: "*The* poorer we are *the* happier we are," he said.
> Relative adverbs: *where, before, while:* We work *while* they play.
> Adverb of manner: She sang *sweetly.*
> Adverb of place: We went *inside.*
> Adverb of time: I'll see you *tomorrow.*
> Adverbs of assertion and negation: *No,* I will *not* go. *Yes,* you will.
> Adverbs of frequency: *Sometimes* I study English.

Auxiliary verb See **Verb.**

Clause A clause is a group of words that includes at least a subject and a verb.

> Independent (Main) clause: *We are studying. We study* because we need to study.

Dependent (Subordinate) clause:

Noun clause: She said *that we must read the book.*

Adjective clause: The boy *who knew the lesson* wrote on the blackboard.

Adverbial clause:
Of time: We shall go *when the bell rings.*
Of result: It was late *so that we had to go home.*
Of reason: I don't know the word *because I didn't study.*
Of condition: I shall go *if you go.*
Of place: We shall go *where we want to go.*
Of comparison: She was *as* happy *as the boy was.*

Complement   A complement follows such verbs as *to be, to become, to seem,* and *to taste.* It describes or renames the subject.

The candy tastes *sweet.*
The girl we saw was *Mary.*

Conjunction   A conjunction connects words, phrases or clauses.

Simple conjunctions: *and, but, or*
Relative adjective: *whose*
Relative adverbs: *where, before, while*
Relative pronouns: *who, which, what*

Correlative   See **Adverb.**

Count noun   See **Noun.**

Degree   Adjectives and adverbs have three degrees of comparison.

Positive degree:
Adjective: He is a *tall* man.
Adverb: She sings *sweetly.*

Comparative degree:
  Adjective: He is *taller* than his brother.
  Adverb: She sings *more sweetly* than I.

Superlative degree:
  Adjective: He is the *tallest* man in.this room.
  Adverb: She sings the *most sweetly* of all.

Dependent clause   See **Clause.**

Direct object   The action of the verb in a sentence is performed upon a direct object:

  I write *letters.*
  He kicked *the ball.*

Frequency words   See **Adverb.** Some common frequency words are: *ever, never, always, sometimes, often, usually,* and *seldom.*

Gerund   A gerund is formed by adding *ing* to the simple form of a verb. A gerund is used as a noun:

  I don't like *singing,* but I like *reading.*

Independent clause   See **Clause.**

Indefinite pronoun   See **Pronoun.**

Indirect object   The action of the verb in a sentence may be done *to* or *for* an indirect object. The indirect object usually comes before the direct object, as in:

  He gave *me* the key.

A prepositional phrase is common for the indirect object when it follows the direct object, as in:

  He gave the key *to me.*

Infinitive   An infinitive is the simple verb form, usually following *to*. It may be used as the object of the main verb in a sentence.

  She wants *to read* now.

Main clause   See **Clause.**

Main verb   See **Verb.**

Mass noun   See **Noun.**

Noun   A noun is a word used to name a person, place, or thing. Mass (or "noncountable") nouns name things that are not usually counted:

> *water, noise, happiness.*

Count nouns name things that can be counted: *book, chair, boy.*

Count nouns may be singular or plural in number:

> Singular number: Nouns are singular when they name one person or thing: *man, glass, piece.*

> Plural number: Nouns are plural when they name more than one person or thing: *men, glasses, pieces.*

Object   See **Direct object, Indirect object, Pronoun.** A preposition connects a noun (or a word or group of words used as a noun) to some other part of a sentence. This noun (or word or words used as a noun) is called the *object of the preposition:*

> He went to *town* yesterday.

Participle   A participle is a form of a verb used as an adjective:

> Present participle: That is an *interesting* story.
> Past participle: I am *interested* in it.

Person   See **Pronoun.**

Phrase   A phrase is a group of related words :

> Prepositional phrase: He sat *in the classroom.*
> Infinitive phrase: We went *to see that movie.*

Plural   See **Noun** and **Pronoun**.

Possessive   See **Pronoun**.

Preposition   See **Object**. A preposition connects a noun (or a word or group of words used as a noun) to some other part of a sentence.

Some prepositions are: *beside, in, in front of, on, up.*

Pronoun   A pronoun is a word that is used instead of a noun:

FIRST PERSON

	Singular	*Plural*
Subjective	I	we
Objective	me	us
Possessive	my, mine	our, ours
Reflexive	myself	ourselves

SECOND PERSON

	Singular	*Plural*
Subjective	you	you
Objective	you	you
Possessive	your, yours	your, yours
Reflexive	yourself	yourselves

THIRD PERSON

	Singular	*Plural*
Subjective	he, she, it	they
Objective	him, her, it	them
Possessive	his, her, hers, its	their, theirs
Reflexive	himself, herself, itself	themselves

Compound indefinite pronouns: *anybody, everyone,* etc.
Indefinite pronouns: *some, any, each,* etc.
Interrogative pronouns: *who, which, what*
Relative pronouns: *who, which, what, that*

Relative   See **Adjective, Adverb, Conjunction, Pronoun.** A relative adjective, a relative adverb, or a relative pronoun connects a dependent to an independent clause.

Sentence   A sentence contains an independent clause which may be connected to other clauses, dependent or independent. It has at least one subject and one verb and expresses a complete thought.

> *John sleeps.*
> *Here is the water which you asked me to give you.*

Singular   See **Noun, Pronoun.**

Subject   A noun (or noun substitute) may be the subject of a verb. The subject performs the action given by the verb.

> *James* threw the apple.

Tense   See **Verb.**

Verb   A verb names an action or a state of being:
> He *kicks* the poor cat. (an action)
> I *am* happy today. (a state of being)

The *main verb* names the action performed:
> He should *see* this book.

An *auxiliary verb* helps the main verb:
> He *should* see this book.
> We *shall have* finished our work by tomorrow.

Tenses:

ACTIVE VOICE

Present	*Present Continuous*	*Present Perfect*
I write	I am writing	I have written
Past	*Past Continuous*	*Past Perfect*
I wrote	I was writing	I had written

Future	*Future Continuous*	*Future Perfect*
I shall write	I shall be writing	I shall have written
I am going to write	I am going to be writing	I am going to have written

PASSIVE VOICE

Present	*Present Continuous*	*Present Perfect*
It is written	It is being written	It has been written
Past	*Past Continuous*	*Past Perfect*
It was written	It was being written	It had been written
Future	*Future Continuous*	*Future Perfect*
It will be written	It will be being written	It will have been written

VOCABULARY

Numbers refer to units. Numbers in boldface type—for example, **3, 8**—indicate that the word is discussed in the text of that particular unit. Words with which the student is probably already familiar are not followed by unit numbers.

Word forms are presented as follows:

Verbs are presented in infinitive, present participle, simple past, and past participle forms. If the simple past tense and the past participle are spelled the same, the last form presented is both simple past tense and past participle.

Nouns are presented in singular and plural forms. If the plural form is spelled simply by adding -s or -es, the noun is spelled out only once. For example, **boss, -es** indicates that the plural of *boss* is spelled exactly like the singular, with the addition of -es: *bosses.*

Adjectives and adverbs are presented in positive, comparative, and superlative degrees. If the comparative and superlative degrees are formed with *more* and *most,* the adjective or adverb is spelled out only once. For example, **afraid, more —, most —** indicates that the comparative degree of *afraid* is *more afraid,* and the superlative degree is *most afraid.*

ability, abilities, 2
able
  to be able to, 2
about
  to be angry about, 7

  to care about, 2
  to forget about, 4
  to talk about, 3
above, 8
accept, accepting, accepted, 3

across, **5**
agree, agreeing, agreed, 5
  to agree with, 11
agreement, -s, 5
air, 9
alike, 9
alive, 4
all, 2
  worst of all, 11
already, 3
among, 8
angel, -s, 6
angry, angrier, angriest
  to be angry about, 7
  to be angry with, 3
another
  one place and another, 14
any longer, 7
any more, 7
anything, 8
anywhere, 1
arm, -s, 13
  arm in arm, 13
around, 5
  around here, 9
arrive, arriving, arrived, 1
  to arrive at, 1
arrow, -s, 3
as
  as far as, 4
ask, asking, asked
  to ask for, 7
  to ask the way (to), 15
at
  at peace, 3
  at the same time, 5
  to laugh at, 8

back, -s
  back of, 10
back
  back and forth, 1
  to bring back, 4
  to move back, 6
  to step back, 6
bark, barking, barked, 4
barn, -s, 1
be
  to be angry about, 7
  to be angry with, 3
  to be found, 13
  to be glad to, 4
  to be in pain, 5
  to be lost, 13
  to be mad, 9
  to be over, 13
  to be proud of, 8
  to be tired out, 15
  to be used to, 3
become, becoming, became, become, 15
beginning, -s, 2
bell, -s, 14
below, 8
berry, berries, 3
better
  had better, 12
between, 8
beyond, 10
bite, -s, 15
bite, biting, bit, bitten, 15
blank, -s, 1
blast, -s, 14
blast, blasting, blasted, 14
blow, blowing, blew, blown, 2

to blow down, 2

borrow, borrowing, borrowed, 4

both, 2

bottom, -s, 5

bow, -s, 3

brave, braver, bravest, 3

bravely, more —, most —, 3

bravery, 3

break, breaking, broke, broken
to break a promise, 7

breathe, breathing, breathed, 14

bride, -s, 13

bring, bringing, brought, 4
to bring back, 4

bullet, -s, 10

bury, burying, buried, 9

but, 1

buzzard, -s, 11

camp, -s, 3

campfire, -s, 3

candy, candies, 14
a piece of candy

card, -s, 12

care, caring, cared, 2
to care about, 2

caribou, 8

cave, -s, 11

certain, more —, most —, 7

chairman, chairmen, 11

chase, chasing, chased, 7

chest, -s, 12

chin, -s, 5

close, closer, closest, 15
close together, 15

cloud, -s, 1

cloudy, cloudier, cloudiest, 1

cobblestone, -s, 13

come, coming, came, come
to come into sight, 9
to come out, 6

comfort, -s, 1

comfortable, more —, most —, 1

comfortably, more —, most —, 1

complicated, more —, most —, 4

conditional, 6

correlative, 15

cotton, 14

count, counting, counted, 2

country, countries
the country, 15

coward, -s, 3

crooked, more —, most —, 12

crow, -s, 9

cry, crying, cried, 2

cut, cutting, cut
to cut off, 8
to cut out, 8

danger, -s, 5

dangerous, more —, most —, 5, 11

dangerously, 5

dark, -er, -est, 13

darkness, 6

day, -s
  in these days, 3
  in those days, 3
  wedding day, 13
dead, 3
deep, -er, -est, 12
  a mile deep, 12
definite, more —, most —, 7
definitely, 7
diamond, -s, 7
different, more —, most —, 9
  different from, 9
disagree, disagreeing, dis-
      agreed, 5
dishonest, more —, most —, 4
distance, -s, 4
do, doing, did, done
  to make someone do some-
      thing, 7
down, 5
  to blow down, 2
  to knock down, 10
drill, -s, 14
  steam drill, 14
drill, drilling, drilled, 14
drop, -s, 2
drown, drowning, drowned, 10
dry, drying, 10
duck, -s, 10
dust, 15
dusty, dustier, dustiest, 15
dynamite, 14

each, 2
  each other, 11

eat, eating, ate, eaten
  to eat up, 4
elephant, -s, 11
emphasis, 7
emphasize, emphasizing, em-
      phasized, 7
end, -s
  in the end, 2
  the end of, 2
ending, -s, 2
engaged, 9
  to be engaged, 9
engagement, -s, 9
Eskimo, -s, 8
especially, 4
event, -s, 7
everybody, 8
everyone, 8
everything, 8
everywhere, 1
examination, -s, 15
examine, examining, exam-
      ined, 15
exception, -s, 12

fall, falling, fell, fallen
  to fall in love with, 13
far, farther, farthest
  as far as, 4
feel, feeling, felt, 8, 14
fence, -s, 1
fight, -s, 7
fight, fighting, fought, 7
finger, -s, 14
fireplace, -s, 1
fit, fitting, fitted, 9

flock, -s, 10
fly, flies, 2
fly, flying, flew, flown, 4
for, 11
  to ask for, 7
  to go (home) for, 10
  to work for (someone), 15
foreman, foremen, 14
forest, -s, 12
forever, 13
forget, forgetting, forgot, for-
    gotten
  to forget about, 4
forth, 1
  back and forth, 1
found
  to be found, 13
fowl, -s, 11
freeze, freezing, froze, frozen,
    8
fresh, -er, -est, 15
fright, -s, 15
frighten, frightening, fright-
    ened, 11, 15
frightened, more —, most —,
    13, 15
from
  out from under, 6
  to run from, 7
front, -s
  in front of, 10
frown, frowning, frowned, 3
fur, -s, 8

generous, more —, most —, 4
get, getting, got, gotten

to get under, 6
to get (things, people) to-
    gether, 14
ghost, -s, 1
gift, -s, 7
give, giving, gave, given
  to give up, 11
glad, gladder, gladdest
  to be glad to, 4
go, going, went, gone
  to go (home) for, 10
  go on, 6
  to go straight to, 4
  to go this way and that way,
    13
governor, -s, 12
great, -er, -est, 6
greatness, 6
greed, 4
greedily, more —, most —, 4
greedy, greedier, greediest, 4
group, -s, 2
grow, growing, grew, grown, 4
  to grow old, 13
  to grow pale, 13
  to grow up, 14

half, halves
  half a mile wide, 12
hammer, -s, 14
hammer, hammering, ham-
    mered, 14
handsome, handsomer, hand-
    somest, 2, 6
have, having, had
  to have an idea, 11

leave, leaving, left, 6
leg, -s, 7
lend, lending, lent, 4
life, lives, 4
lightning, 6
like, 9
like, liking, liked
   would like, 5
listen, listening, listened, 14
live, 4
lizard, -s, 7
log, -s, 9, 12
logger, -s, 12
lonely, lonelier, loneliest, 6
look, looking, looked, 14
loose, looser, loosest, 9
lose, losing, lost, 13
   to be lost, 13
loud, louder, loudest, 12
loudly, more —, most —, 12
loudness, 12
love
   to fall in love with, 13
luck, 2
   much luck

mad, madder, maddest, 9
   to be mad, 9
   to make mad, 9
Maine, 12
make, making, made
   to make mad, 9
   to make someone do some-
      thing, 7
   to make trouble, 2

match, -es, 1
   to put a match to, 1
mate, -s, 15
matter, 15
   What's the matter?, 15
maybe, 15
meadow, -s, 13
medicine, -s, 3
meeting, -s, 11
melt, melting, melted, 8
middle, -s, 9
mile, -s
   a mile deep, 12
   a mile tall, 12
   a mile wide, 12
minute, -s
   Just a minute!, 9
mosquito, -es, 4
mountain, -s, 5
mouse, mice, 11
move, moving, moved
   to move back, 6
   to move on, 14

next
   the next world, 13
nobody, 8
none, 9
no one, 8
nose, -s, 8, 14
nothing, 8
nowhere, 1

of
   in back of (something), 10

on top of (something), 5
out of (something), 5
the end of (something), 2
the other side of (something), 12
this kind of talk, 11
to be proud of (something), 8
worst of all, 11
off
to cut off, 8
old, -er, -est
to grow old, 13
omit, omitting, omitted, 12
on
Go on!, 6
on second thought, 8
on top of, 5
to hold on (to), 15
to move on, 14
to put on, 4
one
one place and another, 14
onion, -s, 2
other, -s
each other, 11
the other side of, 12
out, 5
come out, 6
to be tired out, 15
to cut out, 8
out from under, 6
outside, 1, 6
over, 8, 13
to be over, 13
owl, -s, 13

pain, -s, 2
to be in pain, 5
pain, paining, pained, 2
pale, paler, palest, 13
to grow pale, 13
path, -s, 3
pea, -s, 14
peace, 3
at peace, 3
peaceful, more —, most —, 3, 13
peacefully, more —, most —, 3
perform, performing, performed, 10
performer, -s, 10
pick, picking, picked
picker, -s, 14
pile, -s, 13
pin, -s, 12
pin, pinning, pinned, 12
place, -s
in its place, 7
one place and another, 14
plant, -s, 15
plant, planting, planted, 15
pliers, 9
plow, -s, 2
plow, plowing, plowed, 2
plus, 7
pocket, -s, 7
pond, -s, 10
poor, -er, -est, 3, 6
the poor, 6
poorly, more —, most —, 6
potato, -es, 11
pray, praying, prayed, 3
prayer, -s, 3

prince, -s, 9
princess, -es, 9
print, 12
  in small print
print, printing, printed, 12
prisoner, -s, 5
problem, -s, 11
promise, -s, 7
  to break a promise, 7
  to keep a promise, 7
promise, promising, promised,
  7
proud, -er, -est
  to be proud of, 8
punishment, -s, 5
push, pushing, pushed, 5
put, putting, put
  to put a match to, 1
  to put on, 4

quality, qualities, 10
queen, -s, 9

rail, -s, 14
railroad, -s, 14
rarely, more —, most —, 8
rat, -s, 11
rattlesnake, -s, 5
raven, -s, 8
receive, receiving, received, 10
receiver, -s, 10
redbird, -s, 9
redwood, -s, 12
refer, referring, referred, 2
  to refer to, 2

relative, -s, 3
remain, remaining, remained,
  8
return, returning, returned, 4,
  6
reward, -s, 5
reward, rewarding, rewarded,
  5
rich, -er, -est, 3, 6
ring, ringing, rang, rung, 14
root, -s, 3
run, running, ran, run
  to run from, 7

safe, safer, safest, 5, 11
safely, more —, most —, 11
safety, 11
salesman, salesmen, 14
same, 9
  at the same time, 5
sand, 3
  much sand
say, saying, said
  They say . . . , 12
scar, -s, 3
second
  on second thought, 8
see, seeing, saw, seen, 14
seem, seeming, seemed, 15
sense, -s, 14
separate, separating, sepa-
  rated, 2
separate, more —, most —, 2
  separate desks
separately, 2
sheet, -s, 6

shine, shining, shone, 9
shout, shouting, shouted, 8
sick, -er, -est, 15
side, -s
  the other side of, 12
sight, -s, 9
  to come into sight, 9
simple, simpler, simplest, 4
since, 4
skin, -s, 8
skin, skinning, skinned, 8
sky, skies, 4
smell, -s, 14
smile, -s, 3
smile, smiling, smiled, 3
snake, -s, 5
so, 6
  to think so, 6
soft, -er, -est, 12
somebody, 8
something, 8
somewhat, 9
somewhere, 1
sound, -s, 15
speech, -es, 12
star, -s, 14
stare, staring, stared, 13
starve, starving, starved, 11
steam drill, 14
steel, 14
step, stepping, stepped
  to step back, 6
stick, -s, 15
still, 7
storm, -s, 13
straight, -er, -est, 12
  to go straight to, 4

strap, -s, 10
strong, -er, -est, 6
stupid, more —, most —, 4
success, -es, 8
successful, more —, most —, 8
successfully, more —, most —, 8
such, 12
suggest, suggesting, suggested, 11
suggestion, -s, 11
sunshine, 9
sweet, -er, -est
  sweet tooth, 14

tail, -s, 1
take, taking, took, taken
  to take a trip, 9
talk, talking, talked
  to talk about, 3
  this kind of talk, 11
tall, -er, -est
  a mile tall, 12
taste, tasting, tasted, 14
tear, -s, 4
tease, teasing, teased, 5
tent, -s, 3
that
  to go this way and that way, 13
these
  in these days, 3
they
  They say . . . , 12
this
  this kind of talk, 11

to go this way and that way, 13

those
in those days, 3

though, 15

thought, -s
on second thought, 8

through, 5

thunder, 13
much thunder

thunder, thundering, thundered, 13

thunderstorm, -s, 14

tie, tying, tied, 1, 9
to tie up, 9

tiger, -s, 11

tight, -er, -est, 9

time, -s
at the same time, 5

tire, tiring, tired, 14

tired, -er, -est, 14
to be tired out, 15

tiredly, 14

to, 11
I'll be glad to, 4
to be used to (something), 3
to go straight to (something), 4
to put a match to (something), 1

toe, -s, 15

together
close together, 15
to get (things, people) together, 14

tongue, -s, 14

tooth, teeth
a sweet tooth, 14

top, -s, 5
on top of, 5

touch, touching, touched, 14

toward, 5

trick, -s, 9

trick, tricking, tricked, 9

trip, -s
to take a trip, 9

trouble, -s, 2
to have trouble, 2
to make trouble, 2

tunnel, -s, 14

ugly, uglier, ugliest, 2, 6

uncomfortable, more —, most —, 1

under, 8
to get under, 6
out from under, 6

unhappiness, 1

unhappy, unhappier, unhappiest, 1

unintelligent, 14

unkind, more —, most —, 5

unless, 9

unlucky, unluckier, unluckiest, 2

unsafe, more —, most —, 11

untie, untying, untied, 1

until, 4

up, 5
to eat up, 4
to give up, 11

to grow up, 14
to tie up, 9
upset, more —, most —, 11
use, using, used
to be used to, 3
usual, more —, most —, 3

valley, -s, 13
village, -s, 8

wander, wandering, wandered, 8
war, -s, 3
watch, watching, watched, 14
way, -s
to go this way and that way, 13
to ask the way to, 15
weak, -er, -est, 6
weakly, more —, most —, 6
wedding, -s, 13
wedding day, 13
weigh, weighing, weighed, 9
weight, -s, 9
wet, wetter, wettest, 10
what
What's the matter?, 15
where, 11

whether, 9
whisper, whispering, whis-pered, 6
whose, 4
why, 4
wide, wider, widest
half a mile wide, 12
wildcat, -s, 11
wind, -s, 2
much wind
windy, windier, windiest, 2
wing, -s, 4
with
to be angry with, 3
to agree with, 11
to fall in love with, 13
wolf, wolves, 11
work, working, worked
to work for someone, 15
world, -s, 11
the next world, 13
worm, -s, 11
worst, 11
worst of all, 11
would, 5
would like, 5

yell, yelling, yelled, 6
yet, 3

INDEX